They stared at one an~~oth~~~~er for what~~ seemed like ye~~ars.~~

Finally Poppy shrugged~~, her~~ body defensive.

Oh, sweet mercy.

Innocent. Not just inexperienced but all the way clueless.

The verdict came down with all the weight of a judge's gavel.

Innocent and in his care.

"You're here in my house on my brother's business. I'm supposed to be *protecting* you. Looking out for you. Not taking advantage of you."

"I don't recall you taking advantage of me," she countered somewhat coolly. "If anything, I was taking advantage of you and your experience. I *wanted* that lesson in flirting. And the kiss that came after it."

Innocent *and* curious.

A combination guaranteed to drive Seb insane.

He stepped back fast and put the width of the billiard table between them, praying it would be enough. Innocent *and* his brother's business partner. No casual bedding and walking away under those circumstances. Nothing but complications he didn't need. "I mean it, Poppy. You stay away from me and maybe, just maybe, I'll manage to stay away from you." He gestured toward the door. "Guesthouse is that way. Go."

Accidentally educated in the sciences, **KELLY HUNTER** has always had a weakness for fairy tales, fantasy worlds and losing herself in a good book. Husband…yes. Children…two boys. Cooking and cleaning…sigh. Sports…no, not really, in spite of the best efforts of her family. Gardening…yes; roses, of course. Kelly was born in Australia and has traveled extensively. Although she enjoys living and working in different parts of the world, she still calls Australia home.

Visit Kelly online at her website, www.kellyhunter.net.

Trouble in a Pinstripe Suit* along with *Revealed: A Prince and a Pregnancy* and *Red-Hot Renegade* were finalists for the Romance Writers of America RITA® award, in the Best Contemporary Series Romance category!

*Originally published under the U.K. title *Sleeping Partner*

Cracking the Dating Code is the second story to feature the West family. Look out for future books following this enigmatic family coming in 2013!

Other titles by Kelly Hunter available in eBook:
Harlequin Presents® Extra

*A West Family story

CRACKING THE DATING CODE

KELLY HUNTER

~ Battle of the Sexes ~

Recycling programs
for this product may
not exist in your area.

ISBN-13: 978-0-373-52891-2

CRACKING THE DATING CODE

CRACKING THE
DATING CODE

CHAPTER ONE

TIMIDITY was not an absolute measurement but a relative one. And therein lay the problem. Second youngest of the four West siblings, Poppy had never measured up to any of her nearest and dearest when it came to confidence and the conquering of fear. Didn't mean she was a mouse. Didn't mean she wasn't perfectly functional—just that she preferred book-reading to skydiving and murmured agreement to heated argument. Nothing wrong with that.

Some might even call it sane.

Of course, there were also those who believed she was too shy for her own good and that she needed to step away from her work and get out more and make new friends. As if her admittedly small circle of friends wasn't enough. As if new friends just happened by on a daily basis.

Tomas was a friend. Cryptology mathematician and co-project manager, Tomas brimmed with confidence enough for both of them *and* he understood the language Poppy spoke best. Namely, code.

Tomas had also offered her the use of his private island on which to do some code breaking, with very few questions asked and only one small favour required in return.

Which had been good of him, she told herself over and over as she stepped aboard the *Marlin III* fishing cruiser and politely asked the skipper for a life jacket.

Very, very good of him.

So here she was, back in Australia, her country of birth, with only a boat ride across the open waters of the Pacific separating Poppy from her destination.

Poppy's spray jacket came off and the life jacket went on and then her jacket went back on over the top of that, never mind the skipper's silent amusement. The ocean was not her friend. They were about to travel across it. Nothing wrong with taking a few precautions.

Sunshine. Blue sky. Calm sea. Shiny big boat, manned by the best skipper the bustling Cairns marina had to offer. A boat fully outfitted with GPS and radar and whose skipper had filled out a travel plan sheet in his tiny office, right there in front of her eyes, and handed it to the office manager, who'd pinned it to a board behind her desk. A careful man who took precautions—nothing less would do.

So the journey had started out well, but the clouds moved in fast and so did the wind, and it was against them, making the trip longer, rougher and altogether more unpleasant as the minutes crashed on.

Not that skipper Mal seemed to mind. The lanky, blue-eyed sports-fishing operator proclaimed it an excellent day for a boat ride, and he should know, seeing as he'd worked the Marlin-fishing arm of the family's charter-boat business for the past twenty years. The only issue to concern Captain Mal was their destination.

'Seb knows you're coming, right?' he asked for the umpteenth time.

'Yes,' said Poppy for the umpteenth time. 'He knows.'

'Because I can't get him on the radio.'

'I know.' Mal had been trying to contact Sebastian Reyne every ten minutes for the past hour. *Way to lessen anxiety there, Mal.*

Fisherman Mal had also wanted to put a couple of Marlin lines out and strap Poppy into the fighting-fish chair on the way across, seeing as Poppy was already paying him top dollar for the run, but Poppy had disabused him of that notion fast.

'No, thank you,' she'd told him politely. 'I'm not big on game fishing.' Or any other fishing that required one to actually be on the water. 'I've read *The Old Man and the Sea*. I know how it goes.'

Mal had laughed and told her that the fishing process had moved on somewhat since then, but he hadn't pushed her, and around half an hour into their journey he'd finally twigged that Poppy had a quiet case of rapidly escalating terror on her hands.

'Problems with Seb?' he'd asked, eyeing her sharply as she stood behind him, as close as she could get to the man without assaulting her personal space limits or his.

'Not yet,' she'd said. 'Not that I know of. You know how some people have a fear of heights? I have one of open water. I look at the ocean and it's bottomless and the only way is down. I don't usually travel by boat if I can help it. Unfortunately, it's the only way to get to the island.'

'Couldn't Seb have come to you?' the skipper had asked, and Poppy had smiled at the man through her fear and edged a little closer.

'I'm not going there to see Seb. I don't even know the man.'

Poppy had lapsed into uncertain silence after that, and skipper Mal had ordered her up into the seat next to him and made her pour him a mug of coffee from a thermos, and one for her, too. He had sugar cubes on hand, the old-fashioned kind that horses loved, and he hadn't waited to see if she'd wanted any, just plopped three in her mug and told her to drink up.

He tried conversation, but she didn't have any to spare.

He tried putting music on, but his taste ran to heavy metal, the kind used to rev up the troops right before they opened fire or, conversely, went down in a blaze of glory.

'So what do you do for a living?' he asked. Casual conversation attempt number thirty-eight.

'I write mathematical code,' said Poppy. 'It comes in handy for securing online interactions and the like.'

'You mean cryptology,' said Mal and grinned when Poppy blinked. 'Same as what Tom does.'

'Yes.' Poppy nodded. 'Tomas and I work together— we're in business together. Hence the loan of the island.'

'You're *sure* Seb knows you're coming,' said Mal again.

'I'm sure.' But given that Mal wasn't sure, it probably wouldn't hurt to know a little more about Tomas's reclusive brother. 'Is there something you know about Tomas's brother that I should know?'

'Hard to say,' murmured Mal. 'What do you know about him so far?'

'I know he's wealthy,' offered Poppy. 'I know he and

Tomas bought the island together and that Sebastian designed and built the house on it. But what does he do?'

'Whatever the hell he wants,' said Mal. 'As a rule.'

'I don't suppose you could be a little more specific?'

'Seb's a marine engineer. Heads up a company that runs maintenance on offshore oil rigs. Runs capping and clean-up operations as well. Whether he's running projects from the island is anyone's guess.' Mal turned those wise blue eyes of his in her direction. 'You do realise that no one but Seb lives on this island?'

'I do. But apparently there's a guest house as well as the main house. I'm to have the guest house. Tom's arranged with Seb for it to be fully provisioned. I don't see a problem.'

'In that case, *you* try getting Seb to answer.'

Poppy had no aversion to taking control of radio communications—it helped keep her mind off the seemingly endless blue water all around them. But by the time they reached the island and docked the *Marlin III* at the sweetest little floating pier, nestled within the shelter of a picturesque horseshoe bay, they still hadn't raised a soul and Poppy's nerves had stretched spiderweb thin.

'Seb's quad's here,' said Mal as he tossed her carryall onto the pier and leapt nimbly up beside it before turning back and holding out his hand to haul her up— only Poppy was busy taking the life jacket off and then putting her coat back on. She hesitated before taking skipper Mal's outstretched hand, only the tiniest of hesitations, but it was there and the man noticed it. Nothing personal, wariness was just her way, but she offered up a small, rueful smile of apology and brought out her manners and said, 'Thank you,' as he hauled her up beside him.

Land was Poppy's first thought. Solid, stable land, just a short walk away.

Her second thought concerned Mal's earlier remark. 'You said Seb's quad is here?'

'Over there behind the boatshed.'

'That's a boatshed?' she said of the long, narrow building that began on the beach and stretched a good fifty metres out over the water. 'Looks a little overdesigned.'

'Yeah, well, I'd keep that opinion to myself if I were you,' said Captain Mal dryly. 'It doubles as a warehouse and sometimes an emergency shelter. There's cot space in the loft, a decent-sized cruiser up on rails. I've sheltered there a time or two when the weather's run foul.'

Which the weather looked to be doing rather rapidly, thought Poppy with an anxious glance skywards. 'You're booked to collect me two weeks from today, right? Or earlier if I call you and we can arrange a time that suits. You're booked. I've paid.'

'You're booked, you've paid, and pickup's weather-dependent. Having said that, the forecast isn't showing any big bad.'

'Those clouds don't look big and bad to you?' she asked.

'Nah. They're nothing.' Skipper Mal reached for his pocket and pulled out his phone. Turned it on and showed her his screen saver. '*This* is a cloud.'

No, Poppy was pretty sure that was a cyclone front. 'I'm glad you kept *that* picture to yourself on the way over. Were you out on the boat when you took it?'

'Yep.'

Poppy shuddered. 'Better you than me.'

'You really don't like the ocean, do you?'

'No. Even inland rivers and lakes don't really work for me. But I'm very fond of baths.'

'You mean six inches of lukewarm water in a tub?'

'That's not a bath.' Poppy reached inside her coat pocket for her phone and scrolled through her photos for the rose be-petalled white stone glory of a bath-house she'd visited in Turkey last year. '*This* is a bath.'

Mal snorted. Poppy grinned. Captain Mal was okay. Captain Mal had got her here in one piece.

They reached the side door to the warehouse, a studded metal door with an oversized door handle and an equally impressive-looking lock. Mal greeted it with a loud fist.

No answer from behind the door. Mal reached for the door handle next. It wasn't locked.

'He's very trusting,' said Poppy.

'That he's not,' said Mal. 'Oy, Seb!'

No answer.

They checked the warehouse area. They checked the space where a gleaming white cruiser sat up on rails. He wasn't in the tiny, untidy office.

They found him in the loft.

Sprawled out, face down on one of the cots as if dead to the world.

Mal sighed. Poppy just stared.

And it wasn't just because he had no shirt on.

Sebastian Reyne was not a small man.

His feet dangled over the edge of the bed, and his shoulders seemed almost too wide for it. His jeans clung lovingly to superbly muscled thighs and his butt was taut and round and altogether perfect. And then there was his back.

Sun-bronzed and magnificently proportioned to fit the rest of him, it was a study in the play of skin over musculature and the hills and valleys that came of it. Painters and sculptors would love Sebastian Reyne's back. They'd commit it to memory and drive themselves insane trying to capture every last nuance of its power and beauty.

It seemed only wise that Poppy too should commit such a study in masculine perfection to memory.

Just in case she ever decided to take up sculpting or painting.

Or something.

His chest moved and from what little Poppy could see of his face beneath all that shaggy black hair, his colour seemed good.

An almost empty Scotch bottle lay on its side beside the bed.

Not dead, then.

Just dead drunk.

'Miss West, meet your host,' said comedian Mal as he reached down and gave the sleeping giant a nudge. 'Seb.'

Seb groaned. Muttered something about Mal going away and the words he used were not from the book of manners.

Nothing Poppy hadn't heard before.

'Oy! Seb!' bellowed Mal, and shoved him in the shoulder. 'Package for you.'

'Leave it on the floor,' murmured Seb and his voice rippled over her, darkly delicious and heavy with sleep.

'Yeah, about that,' said Mal, and turned to Poppy.

'Comprehension could take a few minutes. Maybe you should wait in the office.'

'It's okay,' said Poppy mildly. 'I have brothers.'

'Brothers who go on benders?'

'Brothers who do what they want,' she countered quietly, and put her hands to her knees and bent low so as to see Seb Reyne's face. It was quite a face, stubble aside. It put her in mind of fallen angels and very bad boys.

Wouldn't hurt to commit his face to memory too.

'Mr Reyne? I'm Ophelia West. We've spoken on the phone. I'm Tomas's business partner. I'm here to do some work.'

Long, dark lashes lifted a millimetre or two before closing again, giving Poppy a brief glimpse of forest green.

'Am I dead?' he murmured.

'Not quite.'

'You sure?'

'I'm sure.' Poppy straightened and turned to Mal. 'I'm pretty sure he's going to say "Welcome to the island" next.'

Another curse. More of a whimper.

'Give me five minutes with him,' said Mal, and hauled a protesting Seb upright and headed for the door, and then the cove, and then the ocean, dragging the altogether larger Seb along with him.

Poppy stayed on the pier and watched as the pair headed across the sand and into the water until they were both waist deep in it, at which point Commander Mal unceremoniously let the other man go.

Doubtless that would've been her older brother's solution too.

Poppy leaned against the railing as Mal dunked

Seb again, maybe to wash his mouth out this time, but eventually Mal waded back towards the beach and Seb waded into deeper water, scrubbing at his hair and disappearing beneath the surface with the sleekness of a seal.

Definitely not afraid of open water, that one.

'He won't be long,' said Mal when he reached her. 'Seb's had a rough time of it these past couple of months. He lost one of his business partners in an offshore rig explosion. Another one of his crew went deaf in the same accident. Seb blames himself. Did Tom not tell you *any* of this?'

'Not a word.' And there *would* be words between her and Tom about his reticence on the subject. Lots and lots of noisy, robust words.

'You sure you don't want to come back with me?' asked Mal. 'Find some nice little house on the mainland to hole up in?'

'Believe me, I would if I could.' Poppy cut her gaze towards her host, who was in the process of emerging from the ocean, torso bare and body beautiful. She could feel the pull of him from here, the sleekness and the sensuality, and it thrilled and terrified her in equal measure. 'Will I be okay here with him?'

'I can't see him physically harming you, if that's what you mean. Can't see him being overly polite either...'

'What about the drinking?'

'It looks worse than it is,' said Mal flatly. 'He's not drunk. Just tired.'

'From doing what?'

Watching the fish swim by?

Poppy was used to indecision. Not knowing how to

respond to a social situation. Not knowing which instinct to trust—the one that said go back to the mainland with Mal or the one that assured her she'd be safe with this man if she stayed.

Seb was Tomas's brother and Tomas was a friend. Tomas knew when to tease and he knew when to offer up support. He could be a touch protective of her at times. Surely he wouldn't have sent her here if he thought it unsafe? Surely his brother wouldn't be all *that* different?

Seb strode towards them as if he owned the place—which he did—and with a scowl on his face guaranteed to frighten small children.

The scowl didn't frighten her. What frightened her was her response to his nearness. The way she kept taking an invisible tape measure to those broad shoulders, made all the broader by the trimness of his waist. The way she automatically wanted to move closer to him rather than further away, never mind the kick in her pulse and the hitch of her breath. It was the bane of her social interactions, the amount of space she needed to put between herself and others. An arm's length at least. Preferably a table's length. Even with Tomas, whom she'd worked with for over two years now, she kept her distance.

Sebastian Reyne took one last step towards her; Poppy's instinctive step back should have been well and truly activated by now.

But it didn't come.

Poppy took a deep breath, restricted her gaze to anything from the neck up and held out her hand for him to shake.

'Mr Reyne, shall we try again?' she said as quietly

and evenly as she could. 'I'm Poppy West. I believe you're expecting me.'

Beside her, Mal snorted.

Before her, Seb Reyne looked down at her hand and then back at her, his gaze faintly incredulous. 'I'm wet,' he said.

She'd noticed. And she'd been right about his eyes being green. A deep, forest green ringed with grey. 'So you are.'

She made sure there was no judgement in her voice. She wanted that handshake. Reassurance of their business footing, perhaps. A gentle reminder that a man was only as good as his word and that she was here because he'd agreed she could come.

Plus, she had a powerful urge to experience his touch.

His skin was wet. His hand was warm and big, and calloused. One shake and they were done, except for the heat that had travelled like lightning up her arm and through her body and just didn't seem to want to go away.

'How long's this going to take?' he muttered.

'I don't know,' she offered truthfully. 'Anywhere between a couple of days and a couple of weeks. Any longer than that and I'm liable to go bonkers.'

'Aren't we all.' Seb's gaze cut to Mal. 'You're not staying?'

'Can't. Got a charter booked in for tomorrow.'

'Cancel it.'

'Can't. She's all yours, pal.'

'Not quite the wording I'd have used,' offered Poppy mildly. 'However, I am aware that I'll be impinging on you for the duration and that Tomas may not have been fully aware of certain…developments when he offered his hospitality, and yours. Is my staying here going to be a problem for you, Mr Reyne? I was under the impression that it wouldn't be, but if it is…' Poppy shrugged and tried hard not to telegraph dismay. 'Well, it's your island. I can head back to the mainland with Mal.'

Sebastian Reyne ran his hand through his hair and stared out to sea as if in search of a lifeline. Poppy could have told him that lifelines were few and far between out there but she held her tongue and waited for his reply and tried not to let anxiousness overwhelm her.

Mal eyed him steadily—some silent judgement going on there. Poppy tried not to eye Seb at all, which was easier said than done given how much room he seemed to take up.

'I really won't be any trouble,' she said when the silence threatened to snap her nerves completely. 'I just need to work. You'll hardly even see me. That's a promise.'

'If Tom said you can stay, you can stay,' said Seb Reyne finally. 'That all the luggage you've got?' He nodded towards her carryall.

'That's it.'

'Can you drive a quad?'

'I can drive a beach trike.'

'Can you pilot a boat?'

'No. Frankly, Mr Reyne, if it floats you can rest assured I'll hate it.'

'Can you swim?'

'After a fashion,' she offered and glanced towards the ocean horizon. 'But how far and for how long is always the real question, isn't it?'

'She likes baths,' offered Mal laconically, and Poppy smiled, and Seb stared, first at Mal, then at her—as if she'd somehow managed to seduce Mal in the Jacuzzi on the way over in the boat.

No need for Seb to know that no one had *ever* bestowed a femme fatale badge on her before. Or how much she enjoyed the wearing of it, however briefly.

'I need food,' he said.

'Yeah, and I'm on the turnaround,' said Mal. 'You want anything brought back from the mainland when I come to pick her up?'

Seb and Mal headed off down the pier towards Mal's boat. Poppy stayed right where she was. It seemed only polite to afford them a bit of privacy—they were obviously friends. She didn't need to be privy to their every word.

Besides, a little distance might give her time to shake off the aftereffects of his touch and the way that fleeting moment of skin on skin had made her feel. Namely hot and bothered and altogether unsettled.

The wet one was making his way back towards her, his jeans clinging to those long, muscled thighs she'd noticed before.

She hadn't noticed the weight in his crotch before, which given he'd been lying face down wasn't surprising, but she noticed it now and she swallowed hard and looked away.

Probably best not to commit that bit of him to memory. It could quite conceivably spoil her for all other men.

Mal's boat roared to life and reversed away from the pier. Poppy waved and tried to remain calm as her host drew nearer.

'So how do you want to do this?' he asked gruffly when he reached her. 'It's your show.'

'Well…' said Poppy, mindful that his head might well be pounding and his temper short. 'You could always drop me where the computers are, earn my eternal gratitude with a cup of industrial-strength coffee and then leave me to get started on the work I came here to do. Does that sound all right?'

'Yeah,' he said, and shot her a glance she couldn't fathom. 'That sounds fine.'

CHAPTER TWO

SHE wasn't what he'd expected. Tomas had called Poppy a little grey mouse with an IQ several sizes too big for her, but Seb didn't see a mouse when he looked at Ophelia West.

He saw quietness, yes. Adaptability. A certain tolerance for the foibles of others. Calm blue eyes, he saw those too, along with flawless, creamy coloured skin, hair the colour of toffee streaked with sunshine and a lithe, willowy body he had no business noticing.

As for her lips…they'd been the first thing he'd noticed when he'd opened his eyes and he'd known instantly *exactly* where he wanted them.

He should have taken it as a warning.

Hell, he *had* taken it as a warning.

He'd been all set to send her back with Mal, only somewhere along the way she'd treated him as a man of his word and the next thing he knew Ophelia West was staying and Mal was going and everyone was expecting Seb to conjure up a badge of honour out of *nowhere* and be a better man.

Just like that.

Damned if she didn't make him at least want to try.

He headed for the office, found his sunglasses, put

them on and sighed as the light dialled down a notch or four. He tried looking at Poppy West again, mighty relieved when she blended into the surroundings a whole lot better than she had before.

Maybe he'd just been imagining the calamity of her touch and the way her eyes had widened and those angel's lips had parted when his thumb had practically encircled her wrist.

Bacon and coffee. Caffeine and fat. Get those into him, shut her in Tom's office and, if she was anything like his brother, she might not emerge for days.

It sounded like a plan.

He picked up her bag and headed for the quad. Slung his leg over the seat and started it up, wincing at the noisy rumble that played right along with the pounding in his head.

Lots and lots of caffeine and fat.

'You coming?' he said, and without a word she slid into place behind him with her bag in between them like a wall. No hands at his waist, no cheerful flirty quip. Just a colleague of Tomas's who'd come here to work.

It took them fifteen minutes to reach the house.

A fifteen-minute ride along a rough dirt track up the side of a steep hill and along a plateau that today boasted a view of endless ocean blending seamlessly into the hazy blue of an unsettled sky. Wind whipped at Seb's hair and hers and a wayward caramel tendril cut across his cheek before sliding around his neck like a slender hangman's rope.

He gritted his teeth, cursed his wet jeans and asked for all the speed the bike beneath him had.

The roughest patch of track curled around a rock ridge, just before the house came into view. The back

wheels always skidded on slick rock and this time
Ophelia West's hands clutched at his shoulders.

An involuntary shudder rippled through him, not a
prelude to desire but full-blown, roaring lust. Too long
without a woman, he decided grimly. Far too long on
this island alone, with only bleak thoughts for company.

'Sorry,' she murmured and withdrew her hands the
moment the quad found traction again.

'Leave them,' he rasped. 'It only gets rougher from
hereon in.'

This time she set her hands to the waistband of his
jeans, probably under the misguided impression that it
was the better alternative to skin on skin.

It wasn't.

Seb's body took her hands at his waistband as a signal that his jeans would soon be coming *off*.

Fifteen minutes all up, until they stood inside the
house and out of the wind, with Ophelia West looking
around curiously but not saying a word.

Seb should have found her actions reassuring; the
fact that she felt no need to befriend him or force him
into inane conversation.

He didn't.

All Poppy West's silence did was make him want to
know what she thought of the island and of the house.
A house made of concrete and glass and metal. One
that cut into the rock face at its back and enjoyed ex-
pansive ocean views from every room. He'd designed
it himself. Built a fair chunk of it himself too. Took
pride in its rugged beauty and the challenges that had
gone into its design.

Whatever the mouse thought of the place, she wasn't
letting on.

'May I use a bathroom?' she asked and he told her where one was and headed for the kitchen.

Coffee would help. Had to help, and then he'd show her the office, fry up some bacon and then disappear for the day while she did whatever it was she'd come to do and he worked off his hangover, his foul mood, and his awareness of a little grey mouse who was trying hard to be no trouble, no trouble at all, and by doing nothing whatsoever to engage him had captured his attention more thoroughly than anyone had captured it in years.

Seb dumped a wagonload of ground coffee into the shiny stainless steel machine, leaned into the counter and rested his head against a cupboard door.

He closed his eyes and tried to remember what else his brother had said about Poppy West. Tried to remember if Tom had been interested in her, and if so, whether he'd ever acted on that interest.

Probably.

She was exactly his brother's type. Classy. Smart. Kinda sweet, whereas Seb... Seb far preferred his women assured, adventurous and heading towards sinful.

'Coffee smells good,' said a quiet, measured voice, and he straightened and opened his eyes to find her standing uncertainly in the doorway.

'It is.' Was that his voice? That raspy, ill-used croak? 'There's sugar around here somewhere. Long-life milk too. Somewhere.' Probably in a box down at the warehouse. He'd bring some up later.

'I'll take black with one.'

Easy to please, this woman with perfect lips and a planet for a brain.

She'd taken her jacket off and stood there in designer

cut jeans and a dove-grey T-shirt that emphasised fine bones and slenderness. Small, high breasts. Plenty of leg.

A man who wanted a piece of her would have to be gentle; he'd have to take care....

'You want something to eat?' he asked the mouse. *Mousemousemouse.* His *brother's* little grey mouse. Business partner. Whatever. He'd find out soon enough.

'No, thanks. I had a big breakfast.'

Birdseed and yoghurt, what was the bet? 'I'll fill up an Esky for you to take down to the guest house,' he told her. 'There's a fridge there. You'll have to turn it on. Not sure if the bed's made up. I'll get you some linen too.'

He probably should have checked the guest house for spiders. Lizards. Snakes. Gracious hospitality wasn't exactly his forte.

'Change of plan,' he muttered. 'I'll sort the guest house. You just do whatever you've come here to do on the computers. Tom wasn't very specific.'

Ophelia West shrugged. 'It's not very interesting to a layman. But I'd really like to see the computer set-up. Tomas promised me big things.'

'C'mon, then, geek girl. Let's show you what he's got.'

He still hadn't put a shirt on.

Poppy tried to pay attention to her surroundings rather than the man who strode down the hallway in front of her, but it took concerted effort. The house had been built into the cliff face, it seemed, for the rear side wall consisted solely of cool to the touch smooth grey rock. The white ceiling disappeared into it and so did the grey slate floor.

At the end of the hall he opened a door and Poppy followed him into an office.

Generously proportioned, it boasted floor-to-ceiling windows on two sides and a perfect 180-degree view of the ocean. Photos of floating oil rigs and pipelines lined the walls—Sebastian's achievements, one would assume. A framed mathematical proof, written in Tomas's scrawling black hand, stood out amongst them. There was a large draughtsman's table. Two high-end brand-name computers sat on nearby desks.

It was a very nice office, by any standard except the one that mattered most. Poppy stared at the computers, aghast.

'Something wrong?' he asked and she looked up to find Sebastian Reyne studying her intently.

'I hope not,' she said. 'I mean, it's a beautiful work-space, don't get me wrong, and the view is magnificent if you like that kind of thing, but those computers are not what Tomas promised me.'

'What *did* he promise you?'

'Grunt,' she said. 'And lots of it.'

The corner of Sebastian's eyes crinkled, and Poppy paused, mid panic. Gorgeous eyes. Smiley hell-raiser eyes, enjoying a private joke.

'You'd be after the bat cave, then,' he murmured, and crossed the room and opened a door she hadn't noticed earlier. He slipped his hand just inside the doorway, flipped on a light and stepped aside. 'Behold, the promised land.'

Poppy approached the door cautiously, peered inside the room and promptly uttered a favoured phrase she'd picked up from her brothers. And it wasn't *Well, glory be.*

Cooling panels warred with monitors for space. Cable had been built into the walls during the original build, which meant no stepping over it, and memory banks took up almost half of one wall.

Tomas Reyne had built himself a supercomputer.

'This enough grunt for you, Miss West?'

'Poppy,' she muttered distractedly. 'You may as well call me Poppy. I'm going to be here a lot.' She started turning on units, she couldn't help herself. 'Thank you,' she said. 'Thank you for letting me stay.' She stood on the spot and turned a slow circle, taking everything in.

'I take it you have everything you need?' he asked dryly.

Poppy smiled at him, really smiled at the man, and wondered why he blinked. *'Oh, mama,'* she said with utter reverence. *'Yes, indeed.'*

'Are you a gamer too?' asked Seb from the doorway as Poppy began lighting up the various screens. In true geek style, she seemed to have forgotten his presence the second she'd spotted Tom's computer rig. He didn't know whether to be amused or insulted. Eventually he settled on being a bit of both.

'Sometimes I game,' she murmured as she examined one piece of hardware after another. 'You?'

'Sometimes. You ever play with Tom?'

'Mmm-hmm.'

More lights came on, accompanied by the whirring of fans.

'With him or against him?' he asked next.

'Both.'

'Ever beat him?'

'Once or twice.'

'Ever sleep with him?'

Poppy blinked and turned back to stare at him. Cornflower-blue eyes and a world of incomprehension. 'What?'

'My brother. Do you sleep with him?'

'I, ah…no.'

The *no* sounded solid without being vehement. 'Ever want to?'

'*What?*'

That wasn't vehemence either. That was pure and utter incomprehension.

'Don't mind me,' he murmured silkily. 'I'm just trying to figure out what the deal is between you and Tom. Maybe he's got plans for you. It'd help if I knew.'

'Help how?'

'I'd play nice and leave my brother's toys the hell alone.'

He watched her eyes widen and her lips part as the intent behind his words sank in. He watched her gaze skitter over his chest, and then the rest of him, lingering just a little too long over areas that bulged beneath clinging wet jeans and, just like that, all thoughts of playing nice fled.

Warm colour crept into her cheeks and did nothing whatsoever to stem Seb's need.

'I, ah…' She cleared her throat and started again. 'Yes, your brother has plans for me,' she said. 'Big plans. Huge.' Her gaze had dropped below his waist again. Seb allowed himself a tiny smile.

'Really?'

'Oh, yes.'

She couldn't lie for squat. Seb cocked his eyebrow

and shot her a smile and Miss Ophelia West met his gaze and blushed.

'Your brother's waiting for me to become self-assured, playful, sexy and somewhat on the curvy side,' she murmured. 'That's how he likes them, you know? And as soon as I become all of those things I fully expect him to fall at my feet and worship. He's going to let me know just as soon as I meet his requirements.'

'So you'll be having bacon and eggs, then?'

'What?'

'For the curves.' Seb swept his hands through the air, outlining imaginary curves with his hands. They were very buxom curves.

'Oh.' She seemed mesmerised by his hands.

'You want extra bacon?' he said, and smiled a crooked smile.

She shook her head, her smile fey and fleeting. 'No, thank you.'

'I don't think you have any intention of moulding yourself to meet my brother's requirements,' he murmured. 'I think you're waiting for slender, geeky and socially awkward to become the new sexy.'

'It's going to be a long wait.'

'Maybe.' And maybe not. 'Coffee'll be in a pot in the kitchen,' he added. And because he was a gentleman and a good brother and the situation he found himself in required far more consideration than he'd given it so far, 'Get it whenever you want.'

He left her alone after that. Poppy heard the clang of pots and pans in the kitchen and soon enough she smelled bacon frying, but Sebastian Reyne didn't come near her again, and eventually she heard the quad rumble to life. A glance through the window confirmed that Sebastian was indeed heading back down the rough dirt track on the quad, his destination unknown.

He'd changed into cut-off canvas trousers in beige and he'd added a black T-shirt, but it didn't make the slightest bit of difference to her reaction to him. She still looked, and she sure as hell still wanted. She tried to count how many other men she'd wanted with the intensity that she wanted this one. The counting didn't take long.

None.

Poppy retrieved her carryall from the living room and hauled it to the computer room. She dug out her hard drives and plugged them in and then settled down to see what security measures Tomas had put in place. No internet signal was the biggest gift that kept on giving, but there were other safeguards in place and Poppy approved of them all. No way for anyone outside this room to know what went on in here, and as for leaving a mess behind for Tomas to clean up, that wouldn't be happening either. Before she left she'd strip this computer back to this time today, with no record whatsoever of her use of it.

It took a while, but eventually Poppy stopped thinking about her host and let herself sink into the work. No looking over her shoulder required. For the first time in weeks she could truly concentrate on the task at hand. It was time to find out where her older brother was—as in what the hell he was doing and for whom.

'Okay, Jared,' she murmured coaxingly. 'I'm here, I'm fearless and failure is not an option. Where are you?'

* * *

The afternoon stretched into evening before Poppy managed to break free of the code in her head and go to the kitchen in search of that coffee. The unpredictable Sebastian still hadn't returned from wherever it was he'd been going and for that Poppy was surprisingly grateful.

She needed the caffeine and she needed some time alone to think about what she was going to do about her interest in him, and, more to the point, what to do should he continue to display a decided interest in her.

The man was grieving, and probably bored. Looking for a distraction, any distraction would do. A bottle. A woman. Something to take his mind off an explosion that had cost him one friend and injured another. Poppy didn't know what to do with the information Mal had given her. Didn't know what kind of guilt Seb was dealing with or what it was doing to him.

Didn't know whether to act on her instant attraction or leave the poor man alone.

Guilt had been Jared's constant companion too, as they'd sat in plastic chairs in the hospital, waiting for their sister to come out of surgery. Jared's anguish over Lena's injuries had been wordless and all powerful. He'd waited for word that Lena would survive. He'd seen her and spoken to her and told her everything would be all right. He'd sworn vengeance on those who'd betrayed them and then he'd left.

Seven months and twenty-eight days ago.

That was the sum of Poppy's experience of a man consumed by guilt, and if she hadn't been able to help her brother deal with his pain how the hell was she supposed to help Sebastian Reyne shoulder his?

Unless he *wanted* to use her as a distraction?

Flirt with her, get naked with her.

Humour her.

No real emotional connection beyond blind desire for sexual satisfaction. Would that really be so bad?

Because she had the blind desire part of the equation well and truly covered.

Time to raid the kitchen cupboards and nab a couple of biscuits from the biscuit tin. Not making herself at home in Sebastian's home, just ensuring she didn't crash from a mixture of hunger and nerves.

And then came the rumble of the quad bike outside, followed by unhurried footsteps, and Sebastian strode through the door, dominating the space and making it his own.

Which it was.

'I made more coffee,' she said, barely resisting the urge to tuck her hands behind her back, guilty-villain style. 'Stole some biscuits.'

She tried not to get lost in those eyes and that face. Tried very hard to ignore that hard, muscled body so carelessly showcased in castaway clothes.

Tried very hard to play it cool, never mind that her core temperature had just soared.

'You finished for the day?' he asked.

'I can be.'

He came closer, bringing the scent of the sea with him. 'The guest house is ready for you.'

'Thank you. But you're going to have to give me directions.'

'Why don't I just show you where it is? Where's your bag?'

'By the door.' She gulped down her coffee, refilled

the cup with water and set it in the sink. 'Can you give me five minutes with the computers?'

'Are we talking a regular five minutes or the five minutes that magically turns into five hours the minute a computer tragic gets in that room?'

'I'm talking five regular, round-the-clock minutes,' she said. 'Ten at the most.'

'We'll see.' Sebastian headed for the coffee pot and the assessing glance he shot her did absolutely nothing to cool her down.

Resisting the urge to run, Poppy headed for the cave.

She found him ten minutes later, in the garage beneath the house, and followed him back to the quad.

'How far away is the guest house?' Colour her ignorant, but she'd assumed that guest house and main house would be within shouting distance of each other as opposed to, say, opposite ends of the island.

'It's a twenty-minute walk back down the hill. Half that by quad. The guest house sits halfway between here and the boatshed if it's orientation you're after. There's another quad there that you can use to get around the island. It's fuelled up and the same as this one. Get on.'

Poppy got on. Left room for him up front, and the ghost of a smile crossed his lips.

'You're driving. Move up.'

She moved up, tentatively tucking her coat between her legs. Ladylike *not*.

But he didn't seem to notice.

'Key,' he said, his forearm brushing her shoulder as he showed her where it was and she turned it as instructed. 'Foot on the brake.' She did that too, no brushing against him required. 'Kill switch on.' He showed her where it was. 'Now press the start button.'

The engine roared to life and Sebastian slid onto the quad behind her, no carryall in between them this time, for it was slung over his shoulder and, from the looks of it, that was where it would stay. Poppy glanced at him, glanced down at the seat and Seb's strong, long thighs, and swallowed hard. She scooted forward to give him more space. He wasn't a small man, he needed more space.

She needed more space.

She took it slowly down that first rocky, steep bit of track, and she tried to pretend, when his thighs brushed her buttocks, that she'd felt such thighs before and that her heart wasn't about to burst through her ribcage every time a bump in the track slid her into him just that little bit more.

Five minutes down the track he leaned forward, put his lips to her ear and told her to take the fork to the right.

The guest house they came upon a couple of minutes later was a far friendlier version of the big steel-and-glass house. There was still steel, and there was plenty of glass, but the dimensions were smaller and more inviting, and the steepled roof and the generous front deck filled with an assortment of mesh chairs and a hammock had a simple island charm to it that the sophisticated, sparsely furnished main house lacked.

If Poppy's legs wobbled ever so slightly as she got off the quad it was his fault not hers, and if she took one look at his back and stumbled and bit her lip as she followed him up the steps, that was undoubtedly his fault too.

The interior of the guest house was dust free and fully furnished. A king-sized bed dressed in delicate white linens. A white gauze mosquito net hanging from a ring screwed into the ceiling. The netting tucked in behind the pillows for now, ready for sorting out later.

It could be whatever you wanted it to be, a bed like that. A pirate ship or a kingdom ruled by a benevolent princess. A kid would have a ball in that bed, and as for an adult, well…

'What happened to your lip?' asked Seb abruptly and Poppy stopped staring at the bed and touched her fingers to her bottom lip and then stared at them instead.

'Nothing,' she said, for her fingers had come away clean, but his narrowed green gaze seemed fixated on something so she gave her upper lip a once over with her fingers too. 'Biscuit crumbs?'

'You've bitten it,' he said gruffly. 'On the way down.'

'Oh.' Well, yes. 'Only a little.'

Time to cut the tension that whipped through her, and turn away and study the rest of her surroundings rather than him. Poppy didn't know how to play this game of hyper-awareness between man and woman. She had absolutely no idea what to do next.

There were no curtains on the floor-to-ceiling windows and every window was currently open. Fortunately, the windows were screened. A sucker-footed gecko watched her from his place on the whitewashed wall.

'They're harmless,' said Seb, noting the direction of her gaze. 'Bathroom and kitchenette are to the rear, your quad's in the shed out the back and the key's in it.' He set her bag down beside the bed. 'There's fish curry in the fridge and a microwave to heat it up in. Other food too. Hopefully you'll find something you like.'

'Thank you.' Thank-yous she knew how to do. Polite smiles too. Nervousness—she had that one well and truly covered.

'There's no phone in here,' he said next. 'But there is a two-way that'll get you through to the boatshed or the house. If you need to call home, you'll have to come up to the house and use the sat phone. It works most of the time, but not all of the time.'

'You really are quite isolated here, aren't you?'

'Tom didn't tell you?'

'Tom did tell me,' she murmured wryly. 'The reality of isolation just didn't quite sink in.'

'You get used to it,' he said. 'Come up to the house whenever you're ready in the morning. Just go in. Make yourself at home. I probably won't be there.'

'Where will you be?'

'Fishing. Swimming. Rock climbing. Something.'

'Uh-huh.' Man with an almighty need to conquer something. She knew the type. 'Ah, Mr Reyne?'

'Seb.' He waited until he was out of the door before turning back.

Right. Seb. She wasn't sure she trusted herself to say his name right now without layering it full of lust. 'There, ah, don't seem to be any keys to this place.'

'Yeah, we lost them.'

'So how do you lock up?'

'You don't.'

'I *what*?'

'Let me guess,' he murmured. 'You live in an inner-city apartment block surrounded by a million people and you know none of them.'

'You're very perceptive,' she countered lightly. 'I divide my time between Oxford and Sydney. My father's based in Hong Kong. I'm very fond of Hong Kong. Plenty of people. Locks too. Keys.' Not that she wanted to labour the point.

'Relax, city girl. The doors still lock from the inside. Just make sure they're not set to lock when you shut them in the morning. Your stuff will be perfectly safe here, I guarantee it. There's no one else here.'

No one he *knew* of.

'What about pirates? Shipwrecked fishermen? Critters? Blackbeard?'

This earned her a grin, free and clear, and her body responded accordingly. 'If Blackbeard happens by you give me a yell.'

'You are too kind.'

'I know. You got any messages for my brother?'

'You're calling Tomas tonight?'

Sebastian's gaze skittered over her face once more and lingered on her lips. 'Yes.'

'Any particular reason why?'

'Courtesy call.'

'Oh.' Poppy eyed him uncertainly. 'Well, tell him I said thank you for the lend of the island.'

'Anything else?'

Nothing she could think of.

'Miss you… Wish you were here…' he prompted silkily.

'Oh. *That* kind of message.' A message from one lovelorn suitor to another. She had no idea what one would say. 'Yes.' She paused, struck by Sebastian's sudden coiled stillness. 'Tell him I said hello.'

CHAPTER THREE

SEB ate his seafood curry hot and took his bedtime shower lukewarm and stinging. Give it a few days, a week at the most, two weeks at the outside and mousy, brainy little Poppy West would be off his island and so would he.

Head for the mainland. Take care of some business. He found the shampoo—squirted it straight from the bottle onto his hair. Maybe he'd touch base with his crew and then go and lose himself in a woman for a while.

A savvy, experienced, blue-eyed blonde who knew how the game was played and wouldn't expect a damn thing of him other than satisfaction at the time.

Not Poppy West, she of the golden-toffee tresses, cornflower-blue eyes and decidedly enigmatic ways.

Not her.

Seb closed his eyes and scrubbed at his hair, willing his body not to stir, but the more he willed it, the more contrary his body got.

He soaped his chest, took a scratchy sea sponge to his arms.

She'd be pliant in bed; maybe even a little inexperienced.

Deeply, openly responsive.

Seb cursed, a word that had been on his mind all day.

Even if she *didn't* have a thing for Tomas, even if Tom had no interest in her, it would be very poor form to mess around with his brother's business partner.

Tomas, who'd excelled at everything, *including* being a big brother. Pulled Seb out of the pit when his first girlfriend had dumped him for a blue-blooded golden boy. Talked Seb off an oil platform and into an engineering degree. Encouraged Seb's idiot idea of putting together some sort of crack rigging crew. Troubleshoot anything that gushed or burned and cap it, bring it back under control—those were the jobs Seb and his crew took on. Proving his worth, over and over, until finally he'd believed in himself and the things he could deliver. Not as clever as Tomas. Not as polished or urbane, but worth something nonetheless.

Until one crucial split-second decision had cost one man his life and another his hearing.

Seb's crew. Seb's responsibility.

He wanted a drink.

He wanted his friend back.

And in true self-destructive, must-compete style, he wanted his brother's girl.

Seb rinsed off, cut the water and walked naked through to his bedroom. He found a towel, then a pair of loose cotton pyjama bottoms.

He headed for the office and did his best to ignore the faint floral scent that hung in the air there. And then he picked up the phone and called Tom.

'I got your parcel,' he said when Tom answered. 'What the *hell* is she doing here?' Besides torturing him with her nearness.

'Working,' said Tom. 'At least, that's the assumption. Why? What *is* she doing there?'

'Working,' said Seb grudgingly. 'That is not the issue. What *I* want to know is why you sent her here in the first place. You into her? You setting something up? Like a lightning visit?'

'What?' said Tomas.

'God, you even sound like her,' muttered Seb. 'Are. You. Into. Her? It's not a difficult question. A simple yes or no will do.'

'What if I am?' asked Tom warily.

'Then you'd better come and get her before I forget you exist. *Now* do you understand?'

His brother swore, loud and long. Smart man, only, 'I'm not involved with Poppy,' he said at some point during the tirade. 'I have no intention of ever *getting* involved with Poppy,' he said a short time later, and the stranglehold on Seb's chest relaxed. 'But if you think I sent her there for *you* to get into, you couldn't be more wrong,' his brother continued. 'You want to party, get off the island.'

'And leave Her Citified Slenderness here by herself? How do you think *that's* going to work out? She's already nervous about staying in the guest house by herself.'

Silence from Tom.

'Can't she go and work somewhere else?' It wasn't quite a plea for mercy but it was the closest Seb had ever come to one. 'Because if you want me to stay away from her, she's going to have to go.'

'She can't go,' said Tom. 'Trust me on this one. She needs the privacy, the bat cave, and she needs a bit of time. Give her two weeks, Seb. Please. Hell, give her two days. Surely you can manage two days without trying to get her on her back?'

'Crème caramel,' murmured Seb. 'I haven't had a crème caramel in ages.'

'Resist.' Panic in Tom's voice now, but it was too late. Tom didn't want her. Seb most certainly did. 'I mean it, Seb. You treat her like a sister.'

'We don't have a sister.'

'Point taken,' said Tom. 'Then, for God's sake, treat her like my boss.'

Dawn came too early for Poppy, but once the sky began to brighten on the horizon there was nothing else to do but pull the mosquito net aside, turn on her side in the glorious, king-sized bed, find a few pillows to prop beneath her head and give the dawn show the attention it deserved.

Sleep had taken its time coming to her last night. Sunrise took its time too as it stole across the rippling water and then crept across the edge of her bed.

Poppy stretched her hand out to caress it; no bite in the sun's rays yet, but the dust motes in the air glowed silver and they kept her entertained as vivid dreams of making love with Sebastian had kept her entertained throughout last night.

In her dreams, Poppy hadn't been stand-offish or in need of personal space. She hadn't been wary of him or of the things he might do.

It hadn't been awkward. She hadn't been clueless or desperately out of her depth, the way she had been with others.

She hadn't been seventeen going on fourteen and Sebastian hadn't been twenty-two and impatient.

Sebastian hadn't been baffled by her awkwardness or horrified by her age and inexperience when finally she'd confessed it.

He hadn't muttered stumbling apologies interspersed with curses, while scooping up her clothes and directing her to put them on, put them on, before hurriedly showing her the door, saying, 'Sorry, sorry, dear God, I'm sorry. I had no idea.'

Sebastian hadn't said sorry at all.

Fine things, dreams.

Poppy threw her covers back and stretched out and waited until the sun bathed every inch of her in its glow.

Dreams were what wishes were made of.

Sebastian wasn't at the house when Poppy arrived there just on 8:00 a.m. Easy, then, to make herself at home in the cave and find Tom's cache of music and crank up the juice and get down to business.

She almost didn't hear the outer office phone, but the repetitive ring seeped through to her brain eventually and with it came a new dilemma. Answer it or not? Surely the man had an answering machine?

But a quick look confirmed the phone for some sort of satellite affair and whether it had an answering service function was open to speculation. She reached for the phone and picked it up gingerly.

'*Finally,*' said an exasperated female voice. 'I didn't think you were ever going to pick up. You done brooding yet? Because there's a few things here in need of your attention. Like a potential blowout in the Timor Sea. Do we want after it or not?'

'Hello?' said Poppy. 'You'll be after Seb.'

'Who's this?' asked the voice suspiciously.

'*Are* you after Seb?' countered Poppy politely. 'Because I'm quite happy to take a message. I'm quite happy to go and *find* him and deliver a message if it's important.'

'Who are you, exactly?'

'A friend of Tom's.'

'Seb's brother.' The voice grew friendlier by the second.

'Yes. Seb's not in the house right now. I'm not sure where he is, to be honest.'

'In that case, I'd love you to give him a message. Tell him there's a jackup leaking oil and gas in the Montara field. It's been evacuated and I'm pulling in more details from the parent company now. It's a mess. Tell him to call Wendy asap.'

'Tell him or ask him?

'Ask him,' said Wendy. 'But if you can make it sound like it's non-negotiable, all the better.'

'All righty,' said Poppy. 'I'll see what I can do.'

She hung up and, with a wistful glance towards the computer room, headed for the quad and set it chugging sedately down the track towards the boatshed in search of her host.

But he wasn't in the boatshed, so she tried to remember where he'd said he might be as she took the track that ran around behind it and worked the quad slowly around the edge of the island. Fishing, climbing, swimming or something. That was where he'd be.

Poppy kept motoring, with the smell of the bush closing in on one side of her and the smell of the sea on the other, and the colours spread out before her were forest green and azure blue, sometimes butting up against each other and sometimes separated by a strip of sand.

Wind in her hair, the sun on her face and the throb of the quad beneath her. Poppy's senses were sharper here. Her enjoyment of sensual things more pronounced.

Maybe that might explain her fascination with one Sebastian Reyne.

He wasn't on the first stretch of beach that she came to but she did find his quad parked in the shade of some trees on the second. Poppy scanned the beach and the bushland behind her but there was no sign of the man on either.

Sighing, she turned her attention to the sea. Picture perfect, this little blue bay. A semicircle full of shallows and coral clusters and then an abrupt drop off into water of an infinitely deeper blue.

A slight commotion in the water. Darting fins, black tipped and plenty of them. A snorkelling Sebastian, rising from the shallows with a spear gun in hand and a pearly orange fish on the end of it. Spear fishing in the company of half a dozen or so curious sharks.

Man with a death wish, as far as she was concerned, but then, given the day job, what else could she expect?

Poppy cupped her hands and called to him. Waited until he turned around and then stood up and waved him in. Die he would, if that was truly his desire, but please, Lord, not on her watch and not in the water.

He waded back towards the shore and a cohort of black-tipped fins wove in and out around him, but he still had his catch when he reached the sand and stripped off his snorkelling gear, and a grin on his face that spoke of enjoyment, not terror.

'Morning,' he said mildly when he reached her, but Poppy was somewhat beyond a mild-mannered reply.

'You *irresponsible,* self-absorbed d—' Poppy

stopped herself just in time. Settled for glaring at him instead. He wasn't one of her brothers. None of her business if he'd decided that death-by-misadventure was his preferred way to go. Besides, she was only here to deliver a message. And get him off the island. An action that, given the nature of the message, could prove remarkably easy. 'Hi.'

'What was that?' he enquired smoothly. 'I didn't quite catch the last *D* word and now I'm all curious as to what you didn't say. *D* for *daredevil*? *D* for *drunk*? Although I'm not, you'll be pleased to know.'

He stood before her and dared her to pass comment. Man, his mouth, his fish and a lazy, teasing glint in his eye.

'*D* for *dog*? Dirty dog? Because I'd argue that I'm probably quite clean right now. Briny fresh. Or is it the spear fishing you object to?'

'I don't *object* to you catching lunch. Watching you *become* lunch, on the other hand, is a little too out there for me.'

'You mean the reef sharks?' He glanced behind him and there they were. 'Honestly, Poppy, they're harmless. Puppies of the sea.' He'd called her Poppy. Somewhere along the way that bit registered. Puppies and Poppies. Too many *P*'s.

'They like sea urchins best,' he said next and offered up a crooked smile. 'You want to feed them?'

'Feed them?' She knew she was looking at him as if he was mental. That was because he was. '*Feed* them?' He was dragging her attention away from her point. Points in the plural, actually, for she had several of them to make.

Poppy pointed to where the coral beds met deeper

water and waited for the shadow and the fin to reappear and sure enough it did. No darting about for this dorsal fin, or the tail fin that followed some distance behind it—just the slow, smooth glide of a very accomplished predator. 'You planning on feeding that one too?'

Seb's eyes narrowed. The black-tipped reef sharks decided it was time to depart.

'No,' he said slowly. 'Not that one. That one's just passing through. Thanks for the call out though. Appreciated.' He pondered the mysteries of the unknown shark for a little bit longer. '*D* for *dead in the water*?'

'Maybe,' she murmured as the just-passing-through shark ventured into the shallows. Close enough to make out the shape of him, and the dark stripes across his back. A four-metre-long tiger shark, give or take a little refraction error on account of the water. She could be calm now that Seb was out of the sea. Calmer, at any rate. 'Big, isn't he?'

'Yeah,' he said.

'Ever thought about stretching a nice little shark net across the mouth of the cove?'

'Not 'til now.'

The shark was moving slowly away, cruising the far shallows and finding nothing of interest. Sharks were very distracting. Time to get back to the point. The other point. 'Wendy rang. She wants you to ring her back. She said, and I quote: "There's a jackup leaking oil and gas in the Montara field." It's been evacuated and she's getting more details from the parent company. Is it just me or is that shark looking for something?'

'It's just you.'

'Excellent. Did I mention the bit about Wendy wanting you to call her back?'

'Yes. Did she say who the parent company was?'
'No.'

'Figures. Now she knows I'll ring her back.'

Seb stood watching the shark through narrowed eyes, more sombre now than he had been before. Thoughtful man, working his way through a world of offshore trouble and a little reality check that paradise did indeed have its serpents.

Or maybe he'd known that all along.

'I'll just...head back,' she murmured. Probably for the best. Otherwise she might be forced to commit to memory yet another close-up view of all that rippling muscle and sun-browned skin.

'You go ahead. I'll be up in a minute.'

Not a lot of urgency about him but then maybe he didn't have cause to be. Maybe getting ready to go cap an offshore oil rig took time. She glanced at the shark again. Resisted the urge to step a little closer to Sebastian. It was a very strong urge and it took her by surprise. Poppy rarely had the urge to step closer to anyone. Probably the presence of the shark. Nothing whatsoever to do with the way Seb himself seemed to slide right past her defences as if they didn't exist. 'Looks like he's getting ready to leave,' she said.

'They do that.'

Hard to tell if Sebastian was all front, dry fact or a bit of both.

'One more guess,' he said as she headed for her quad, and there was something altogether dangerous in the smile he aimed her way. '*D* for *dashing*? *D* for *daring*?'

'No,' she murmured dulcetly. 'The closest *non-D* word I can think of is *idiot*.'

* * *

Seb stayed on the beach for another five minutes or so after Poppy made her exit. He didn't want to tail her all the way back to the house and he didn't want to drive in front of her and leave her behind. Far easier to stay here and gut and scale his coral trout and get a grip on what he might say to Wendy when he finally got back up to the house and made that call. He'd want details, that was a given. He'd want to know whose drillships were nearby and who else, if anyone, was in a position to do the work. Maybe even the parent company could do it.

Which was just fine by him and a hell of a lot cheaper for them.

Seb made it back to the house eventually. He slid his catch in the fridge and slapped a bit of cheese between two slices of bread by way of lunch and wondered about making Poppy a cheese sandwich too. In the end he decided yes, she'd taken time out of her day to come and find him, and if she was as besotted by numbers and computers as Tom was, and as desperate to get her work done as Tom suggested, it would have cost her to drag herself away from it.

A cheese sandwich for little Poppy, then, and a coffee to go with it, and he set them down on the drawing board in the office, and called to her the way he'd call to Tom.

'Lunch,' he said and she came out of her cave and shot him a wary smile and thanked him and took it back inside.

Obsessive.

When it came to her work, Poppy West was highly predictable.

His reaction to her presence was highly predictable too, but he'd toned it down—heaven help him, he had. Two days, maybe he could even manage three, and then he'd get them the hell off the island and then they would see.

Seb sat at his computer, took a sip of his scalding black coffee, closed his mind to the indecision that plagued him when it came to both his work and the woman currently running his senses ragged and set about making a few calls.

CHAPTER FOUR

HE'D brought her lunch.

The plainness of the fare shouldn't have set Poppy's stomach to fluttering, but it did, and Seb's continued presence in the outer office as he spoke on the phone only made it flutter more. She heard him asking for details, and she got up and put Tomas's headphones on and caught Seb's eye as she half shut the door.

Shutting it completely was a very bad idea given the hardware in the room and the potential for overheating, but an earful of music she could do, and in doing so give him privacy in which to work and hopefully make him feel happier about her continued presence.

Easy to lose herself in her own work after that, and the challenge of a cipher that wasn't designed to be broken without the right key.

The solution was very simple.

All she had to do was figure out what that right key might be.

It didn't seem more than twenty minutes before Seb was knocking on the half-closed door, and Poppy looked round at him with a frown.

Seb rolled his eyes and approached her chair. Lifted one of her earphones and said in her ear, 'It's six o'clock,

Poppy. You planning to work through the night or are you going to come and eat?'

Well, when he put it like that…

Poppy stood and stretched, and decided to let her latest attempt at cracking this thing keep on running. As for her hyper-awareness of Sebastian, it was still there, but running alongside it now was the surprising notion that she felt quite comfortable in his presence, in the same way she felt comfortable around family.

Not shy or awkward, or worse, trying not to be shy and becoming even more awkward. Just…he was treating her as if he already knew her ways and didn't find them odd. No comment, no questions that made her feel like a freak—he just took her in his stride. How long had it been since anyone other than family had simply taken her in their stride?

Points for Seb. Especially seeing as she hadn't taken his eccentricities—like swimming with sharks, for example—in her stride at all.

'What happened with the oil spill?' she asked.

'Not a lot. AMSA's going to try and contain the slick but there's no getting back onto the rig to do any assessment at the moment. It's too dangerous.'

'Who's AMSA?'

'The Australian Maritime Safety Authority.'

'Will you get involved at a later date?'

'Probably not. This particular parent company has the resources to do their own dirty work. We're closer, but no one's getting near the leak any time soon anyway. Cheaper for them to mobilise a drillship and a crew out of Singapore, even if it does take five weeks for them to get there. We'll stay in the loop, though. Could be we'll be needed. How'd your work go today?'

'Bad.' They'd reached the kitchen and suddenly she was starving. 'What are you cooking?'

'Fish stew.'

'Like last night,' she murmured.

'Not like last night at all,' he said, deadpan. 'I added beans.'

Poppy smiled as she peered into the pot of fragrant, coconut-milk-laden stew. Man was a comedian. 'What else do you do around here for entertainment?'

'Are you flirting with me?'

'No.' Her powers of flirtation had always been non-existent, ask anyone.

Not that Sebastian needed to know any of that. He was to some extent a clean slate. He didn't know much about her at all.

'Because you can if you want.' He shot her a crooked smile. 'Feel free.'

'You want me to flirt with you,' said Poppy slowly.

'Only if you feel like it. Something to pass the time. Besides, it's good practice.'

'Practice?' The beginnings of an idea flitted through Poppy's brain. Poppy prided herself on being good at what she did. The best. And when it came to her work, a combination of natural aptitude and a great deal of practice had put her at the top. Could her uselessness at flirting really be addressed that simply? 'You think I need practice?'

'Hard to say,' he murmured. 'Do you?'

'Maybe.' Maybe a lot. 'My sister, Lena, tried to show me how to flirt once. It didn't end well.'

'For you?'

'For him. We were practising on the same boy, Trig, who's a friend of my older brother's. I wasn't really in-

terested in him and neither was Lena. He was just—'
Poppy waved her hand in the air '—there. In hindsight,
we should probably have *told* him we were only practic-
ing. We probably should have mentioned it to Jared too.'

'Wonderful thing, hindsight,' murmured Seb. 'Let
me guess. Trig flirted back with one of you, or both of
you. Either way, your brother beat him up.'

'No, Trig ignored us for all he was worth and *Lena*
beat him up.'

'Poor Trig. I appreciate his dilemma,' offered Seb.
'What did he do next? Run?'

'No, he joined the special intelligence service. So did
my brother. So did Lena, a year later. Trig and Lena's
arguments have escalated somewhat since then.'

'Wonder why?' murmured Seb.

'Don't we all.' Poppy smiled impishly. 'Trig worships
the ground Lena walks on—not that he ever *mentions*
it. The hope from those in the front-row seats is that one
day Lena will realise it, return the favour and put him
out of his misery. Not that Trig seems miserable. I think
he's enjoying it. You're a man—how does that work?'

'Ever been Marlin fishing?'

'No.'

'I'll give you a clue. Lena's the fish.'

'Ew.'

'So what does your older brother think of Trig's
dilemma?'

'Hard to say. Jared's missing. No one's heard from
him in nearly eight months.' Poppy shoved her hands
in the pocket of her cotton trousers as all thoughts of
flirtation fled. 'Are you hungry? I'm hungry.'

So he ladled stew into bowls and they ate standing

at the counter and after that Seb offered up the island's repertoire when it came to entertainment.

'There's a sudoko tablecloth around here some-where,' he said. 'I could fish it out for you?'

'No. I'm all numbered out.'

'Game of 3-D chess? You'll win. I'll lose. I'll get over it.'

'If you already know you'll lose, there's no point playing.'

'There's a billiard table,' he offered.

'That could work,' she said. 'Movement would be good and it's not too taxing on the mind. I estimate I have a good half an hour of billiards in me before cata-tonia takes hold.'

'Well, hell, Miss Ophelia,' he drawled, and this time that reckless smile of his came out in full. 'If it's an in-tellectual challenge you're after, I could always teach you how to flirt while we play.'

Half-six saw them in the billiards room, with the wind picking up outside and whitecaps dotting what they could see of the ocean. Which was plenty. Every room in this house had floor-to-ceiling windows and that breathtaking ocean view. They'd put the music on. A little bit of good ole boy rock, a little bit of southern-fried bluegrass. Poppy's billiards beverage of choice was lemon-barley cordial. Sebastian had opted for max-imum-kick cola. Both drinks were over ice. For now, at any rate, it appeared that Sebastian's dance with the whisky bottle was done.

'So we're in a bar,' said Sebastian conversation-ally as he chalked his cue. 'And you see someone you wouldn't mind getting to know a little better. What do you do next?'

'So…you really *are* trying to teach me how to flirt?' asked Poppy tentatively.

'Just seeing what you've got.'

'Oh.' A smile spread through Poppy before she could stop it. It was the smile of a child who'd suddenly been given free run of the toy room. She couldn't flirt to save herself and she needed to practise, preferably somewhere private and with someone who was willing to teach her. An expert in the field. A person she didn't recoil from. Someone who didn't know how clueless she was when it came to this sort of thing.

Learning opportunities didn't come much brighter than this.

'So we're in a bar and I see someone I wouldn't mind getting to know a little better,' she echoed thoughtfully, studying the break, which had been hers only it hadn't exactly gone her way. 'Do I know this person already?'

'Assume no. What do you do next?'

'I make eye contact,' she said, making very good eye contact with the black.

'And?' he prompted.

'Smile like I mean it.'

'And?'

'Isn't that enough?'

'Don't you want to check out who he's with?' he asked.

'Wouldn't I have done that first?' Sebastian leaned in to take the shot, his shaggy hair glossy black beneath the table light. 'Made sure he wasn't part of a couple?'

'Depends,' he said. 'You might not care.'

'I care,' she murmured. 'I'm looking for a wedding

ring. If he has one, I'll move on. If he has a boyfriend, or a girlfriend, grandparents or children with him, I'll move on.' Poppy paused, and shot Seb a very level stare. 'He has a wife, three kids, and a mother-in-law who's not impressed. I'm turning away. Scanning the room for someone else I'd like to get to know.'

'Good.'

'There isn't anyone.'

'Now is not the time to be picky,' said Sebastian. 'You're there to flirt, not marry the guy. Keep looking.'

'All right, I've found one.'

'What's he look like?'

'Interesting. He favours black, he's drinking Limon-cello and I like the spider-web tattoo on his skull. I feel I could use it as a talking point.'

'Move on,' said Sebastian, sparing her a quelling glance before sinking another solid-coloured ball.

Poppy blew her fringe from her eyes the better to admire his technique. 'The barman's kind of cute. Nice eyes. Brown. Smiley. Besides, I need a drink. This is nerve-racking.'

Holding her own in conversation with Seb was indeed nerve-racking, but there was a certain freedom that came with imaginary flirting. Action without consequence. A safe learning environment. Poppy smiled.

'Ouch,' murmured Seb. 'Killer smile. There's something almost joyous about it. Innocent even. The barman's heading your way at a dead run.'

'Really?'

'Never doubt it.'

'What do I do now?' she asked.

'Tell him you're in the mood for a single malt whisky, hold the ice. Ask him what he recommends.'

'Is that your preferred poison? Whisky?'

'Usually.' Those green eyes of his were assessing. 'Am I detecting a note of censure? Are you after knowing if I have a drinking problem?'

'Do you?' she asked quietly.

'No. The way you found me the other morning was an exception, not the rule. Not that you have any real reason to take my word on that. You're just going to have to wait and see.'

Poppy shrugged. 'For what it's worth, I believe you.'

'Trusting,' he murmured. 'I'm starting to fear for your safety.'

'Don't be afraid,' she said. 'I'm asking for something with gin in it. The barman's suggesting either a gin fizz or a pink lady. I really don't like either. I think it's a sign. We may not be compatible.'

'It's not a sign. It's a compliment. Tell him you're not that sweet, give him another taste of that lethal smile and try not to lose eye contact. And don't blush. You have a tendency to colour up when you're thinking naughty thoughts and the minute you do you lose any advantage you might have gained.'

'Maybe I *want* to lose the advantage,' she offered mildly. 'Maybe keeping the upper hand isn't as important as making a connection. Maybe I'm inclined to look kindly on a man who can make me blush.'

'You're leaving yourself wide open,' he muttered grimly. 'I don't like it.'

'Well, fortunately, I'm not flirting with you,' she countered coolly. 'The barman's offering to make me a Tom Collins. I've told him that's perfect. He's asking me if I'm new in town.'

Poppy studied the table, lined up the shot and sank

it in one smooth movement. She could feel Sebastian's gaze upon her but she didn't look up. 'I have his attention and you're right. I don't want to be too trusting or too naive. No one likes getting hurt.'

'Finally she sees reason,' he muttered. 'Tell him you're just passing through. Ask him where's a good place nearby to go and eat.'

'What if I'm not hungry? What if I live nearby?'

'Nobody's saying you have to eat *now*. And you do *not* say you live nearby. It's an opening. The barman will know what to do with it.'

Poppy played another shot. Striped ball to side pocket, with the white spinning off exactly where she wanted it.

'Where'd you learn to play?' asked Seb suspiciously.

'My brother's beach house. It's his wet-weather entertainment when he's really bored. We play for favours. He currently owes me three bathroom cleans and a deck oil.'

Her next shot ran fractionally wide of the pocket. Poppy sighed. This was what she got for paying attention to the breadth of a man's shoulder and not the ball.

'The barman's giving me a bar menu. He's moving away. No impromptu invitation to dine is forthcoming. He's not interested.'

'He's making your drink. Relax, he'll be back.'

'Probably to take my fish and chip order,' said Poppy. 'I'm all flirted out. The barman did not make me blush. You think he could make my Tom Collins to go?'

'This isn't working, is it? I'm not sure the barman was such a good choice for you. Let's assume he gives you your drink and you pay him and return to your table. Some work colleagues are with you. Tom's there and he's smiling at you. What do you say?'

'Why aren't you at work?' she said immediately.

'Well, it's a start,' he muttered dryly.

'The gin is gone,' said Poppy. 'And there's no way I'm flirting with Tomas. I'm sorry to have misled you earlier, but I can't do it. I value my working relationship with your brother far too much for that. He'd be impossible to replace. Flirting with Tomas is out. Even in an imaginary bar.'

'Bear with me,' said Seb. 'Tom's brother's just walked in. Tom's introducing him to you. What do you do?'

'So…you want me to flirt with *you* now?' Poppy eyed Sebastian uncertainly. 'As in here by the billiard table? Or are we still in the imaginary bar?'

'Doesn't bother me.' Sebastian's grin came slow and easy and laid waste to any sensible conversation Poppy might have thought to be going on with.

'I think the bar,' she murmured. The bar was not real, ergo any flirting she attempted in it was not real either. 'You go first, though. I'm too busy staring at you and coming to the conclusion that you're a lot bigger than your brother and a great deal more—'

'Docile?' he offered.

'Disturbing. I'm sensing you swim with sharks on a regular basis. Laugh in the face of gushing oil wells. Break hearts every other day.'

'You don't know that yet.'

'*Do* you break hearts every other day?' she asked.

'Not if I can help it. This is a point in my favour, I might add.'

'I'm also trying to figure out if you're already in some kind of romantic relationship,' she murmured.

'You're not wearing a ring, but I'm sceptical about your being unattached. I think I'm going to pass.'

'I'm unattached,' he said. 'Tom's probably told you this in passing. I'm asking you what you're drinking and whether you'd like another.'

'I'd like a mineral water this time, with a slice of lime.'

'You realise the addition of lime pegs you as high maintenance?'

'Does it? Maybe I am.'

'You're really not.'

'Then it'll come as a pleasant surprise to you later on. The lime stays.'

'Recalcitrant,' he murmured.

'Maybe you like that. I can see a wayward woman appealing more to you than a mousy one. I'm all for ditching my current mousy image.'

'Really?' He stared pointedly at her light blue short-sleeved T-shirt and slimline grey trousers. 'What are you wearing?'

'An outfit I got for Christmas. A baby-doll black dress and a bone-coloured shortish trench coat over the top of it. It's the sexiest outfit I own.'

'A trench coat is the sexiest outfit you own,' he echoed with a glum shake of his head. 'That's just sad.'

'Never underestimate the transformative powers of couture, Sebastian. I did not choose this outfit. My very savvy, very confident, soon-to-be sister-in-law chose it for me. That woman can rock a room just by stepping into it. I look good.'

'All right, I've noticed. Now what do you do?'

'I ask you if you've ever played billiards in a steel and glass fortress on a deserted island in a storm before.' Because the wind was of a certainty picking up and the clouds were on the roll.

'I say yes.'

'Who won?'

He sank two more balls in rapid succession and lined up the third. 'Me.'

'You've played this game before,' she said and he cut her a glance and sighed.

'That's it? That's all you've got by way of flirty words?'

'And you smell very nice too. I noticed it before. You smell like the sea.'

'You hate the sea.'

'I like the smell of it. Always have. And I'm fresh out of flirty words. I think I'm just going to stand here now and look good. See if that suffices.'

'It won't. Why don't you try a few flirty moves?' he suggested helpfully. 'At the next gust of wind, flinch and move a little closer. I'll probably ask you how you're holding up.'

'Are you sure that's a good move for me?' she countered with a frown. 'It seems a little needy.'

'I like being needed.'

'Don't we all. I just don't see why *I* have to be the needy one. I'm all for equal neediness or none at all.'

'All right, ditch the damsel in distress play, although for future reference it could really work for you. We're moving on to vamp. You're going to try channelling Marilyn Monroe. In a trench coat.'

'Couldn't I try channelling Mae West instead?'

'Well, you *could*, but then you're going to need a few good one liners and you don't have any.'

True. Poppy sighed. 'All right. What would a speechless vamp do?'

'She'd station herself right where I'm going to want to stand next. Look at the table, read the play.'

Finally something Poppy could do with ease. She moved. Seb played the ball. White ball to Poppy. Maths was very predictable.

Men, on the other hand, were not. Rather than head towards her, Seb headed for her drink, picked it up and brought it over to her.

'Touch my fingers as you take it,' he instructed.

Poppy did so. Sebastian smiled. 'Now you have *more* of my attention,' he murmured, with his lips to her hair and his chest brushing against her shoulder as he turned back towards the table.

Poppy's shoulder tingled where he'd brushed it; the heat of him warmed the air between them.

'You are deliberately invading my personal space,' she said.

'That's the point. If you don't like it, move away. If you do like it, let me know by turning in to me rather than away from me.'

'What do I do with my drink?'

'Good point.' He took it from her and put it back on the bench and then returned to stand beside her, smiling as he took a strand of her hair between his fingers and tucked it gently behind her ear.

'What was that for?' she whispered breathlessly.

'Maybe I thought it was in the way. And maybe I just wanted to touch you. See if you responded.'

'How'd I do?'

'Well, I'm liking the parted lips and the indrawn breath. Not sure you can improve on any of that. However, in the interests of being a true gentleman

I'm now going to take a step back and concentrate on the table, and see what you do.'

'I wouldn't move away? Give you some space to play the shot?'

'Not if you wanted more of me.'

'If I *did* want more of you, what would I do?'

'You move closer to me. Let your shoulder brush up against mine, yep, that'll do it, elbow to elbow as well, and now you study the play.'

'It's not an easy shot,' she said.

'I know. How about you offer me a little wager against sinking it?'

'Ten dollars says you won't.'

'A kiss from you says I will.'

Poppy drew back, just a little, just to see if he was serious.

'Flirt,' he reminded her with a trickster's grin.

'Done.' What the hell had she done?

'*Now* you can move out of the way,' he said and turned around and sank the ball.

Silence would have reigned supreme except for the play of the music and the thumping of Poppy's heart. 'You're not really expecting a kiss from me, are you?' she asked warily. 'In the here and now?'

'Depends on just how far you want this flirting lesson to go,' he countered easily. 'You could always offer to clean my bathroom instead.'

'I'll take the kiss. It'll be over faster.'

'That's one way of looking at it.'

There were other ways to look at a kiss from this man, however, and Poppy was fully aware of them. Call it research or call it practice. Call it whatever she wanted, she wanted to feel Sebastian's mouth on hers.

Courage in hand, Poppy set her hands to Seb's chest, leaned forward on her tippy toes and kissed him.

Sebastian didn't know what to expect from the touch of Poppy's lips on his, but it wasn't this. He meant to pull away, put a stop to the flirting and the kissing and turn the conversation to safer topics, like the weather, or when she might conceivably get her work done so that they could both get off this rock and back to civilisation, so that he could take care of a few things—like the taming of his libido.

But meaning to do something and actually doing it were two different actions altogether.

Ophelia West's lips were full and soft and no power on earth could have stopped Seb from coaxing them open. Slowly. Gently. One tiny stroke of tongue at a time, and her taste when finally he tasted her made him groan on account of the sweetness. He gripped the edge of the billiard table with his hands, no pressure on her to continue this, no pressure at all. Just in case she *was* an innocent. He had a feeling....

He couldn't tell.

When her tongue tentatively met his he let her play and he played with her in turn. Encouraging it. Half wild for it.

Poppy's hands crept up to his shoulders and then to the hair at the back of his neck.

He didn't mind.

Seb closed his eyes, opened his mouth and feasted. Slow and languid when he remembered to be. Hungrily demanding when he forgot.

He forgot a lot.

She edged closer, and with one hand still clinging

to stability he put his other hand to her waist and drew her closer still. Gentle, until he forgot and hauled her against his rampant, rigid hardness with a groan.

Her indrawn breath came quick and shaky. Absolute stillness came moments after that.

Seb kept his eyes closed and his curses to himself as Poppy's hands left the back of his neck and her lips left his.

He drew his hand back from her hip, took a death grip on the table behind him and opened his eyes. Remembered to breathe.

Cornflower-blue eyes stared back at him, stunned.

Silent apology soon followed, although what she thought she had to apologise for was anyone's guess.

'I, ah...probably shouldn't have done that,' she said faintly, and pushed off him completely and there was space between them now. 'You're very kind.'

He had occasional, brief moments of kindness. Not sure this was one of them.

'To humour me and let me practise on you. Like that.' A fluttering wave of her hand supposedly told him what she meant by *that*.

'It wasn't a hardship.' Damned if he had the concentration for playing games now, not with desire riding him this hard. 'Please tell me you're not a complete innocent. That you've had at least *some* experience when it comes to kissing and all the rest.'

They stared at one another for what seemed like years.

Finally Poppy shrugged, every line of her tidy little body defensive.

'Some.'

Oh, sweet mercy. 'How much?'

'I'm not a child, Sebastian.' Her mouth set in a mulish line. 'Enough.'

He tried to believe her. He wanted to believe her. But he just couldn't shake the notion that Ophelia West was innocent. Not just inexperienced but all the way clueless.

Or was she?

'So what happens now?' he murmured. 'You want to continue where we left off?' Because his body most certainly did, even if his brain was ringing a warning bell or ten.

'I, ah...'

Innocent.

Or just undecided.

Did it really matter which?

Sebastian tried to put himself in Poppy West's shoes. A woman here to work, who'd stumbled onto some play by accident and wasn't sure if she wanted to proceed. A woman, moreover, who was dependent on him for food and shelter and had no way off this island for now. If those were the issues running through *his* brain, heaven only knew the kind of thoughts that might be running through hers.

'Tell you what,' he murmured, 'why don't we just chalk this one up to capricious winds and start afresh with each other in the morning? As in "Hi, I'm Seb, Tom's brother, and I'll be your host while you're on the island."'

Poppy stared at him uncertainly.

'Now your turn,' he prompted. 'Something along the lines of "Hi, I'm Poppy. It's not really my mission in life to drive you to distraction. I just stumbled onto that one by accident."'

Uncertainty turned to tentative amusement. 'Consider it said.'

'No, you have to say it.' Time to put the width of the billiard table between them and pray that it would be enough. Because the slightest hint of encouragement and his resolve to play the chivalrous host would be well and truly tested. 'What's more, you have to sound like you mean it.'

'Hi, I'm Poppy,' she said. 'I thank you for your hospitality, the flirting lesson and the kisses. The kisses were…'

'Delicious?' he prompted. 'Delightful? Don't say disastrous.'

'I wasn't going to say disastrous,' she murmured.

'Compliments will get you everywhere.'

She liked that. She didn't run with it—inexperience rearing its head again? But she liked it.

'Be that as it may,' she said, 'I'm going to turn in now because I'm a little bit out of my depth with you.'

'Only a little?' He couldn't help it, he had to know.

'It doesn't have to be a lot,' she countered. 'If I can't touch the bottom and I can't swim to safety I'm still going to drown. So here's me—swimming to safety and saying goodnight.'

'Smart,' he told her. 'I heard that about you. Goodnight, Ophelia.'

'Goodnight, Sebastian.'

But she didn't seem inclined to move.

Seb inclined his head towards the door. 'Guest house is that way.'

Poppy flushed pink and shielded her eyes with her lashes. She put her billiard cue gently down on the table.

And then she fled.

* * *

Poppy roared down the dirt track with scant regard for her safety or the fast approaching dusk. Mortification rode with her, an insistent companion, as she replayed the evening in her mind, trying to figure out how things had gone so wrong.

There'd been the meal, which she'd thanked him for.

The billiards game, which she'd been losing.

The flirting, at which she'd been hopeless.

And then there'd been the kiss.

Yep, the root cause of the problem had been the kiss. She'd been completely enmeshed in it, sensory overload.

And then he'd pulled her closer and she'd felt his arousal and the enormity of what she was doing—of where Sebastian's greedy, knowing mouth was leading her—had crashed down on her. She'd wanted to be ready for more but she hadn't been.

Inexperience had rendered her motionless. Speechless.

Shocked.

But not unwilling. He'd read her wrong if he'd read her that way. She just hadn't known how vividly arousing close body contact could be.

And now she did.

The quad throbbed beneath her but it wasn't enough.

Seb had noticed her inexperience. Picked it, pegged it, been horrified by it and, yes, age-for-experience she was in the minority, but she was open to change and always had been. She'd just never found the right vector for it.

Before now.

Poppy kept on driving and minutes later parked the quad in the little shed behind the guest house and made her way up the back steps, through the wet room and into the tiny kitchen, turning the light on as she went. A sucker-footed gecko skimmed along the wall, taking refuge behind a cupboard, tail in and nose out.

Poppy leaned down, hands on her knees until she spotted half an eye and then she spoke.

'He kissed me, gecko. No one has ever kissed me like that before. It was...'

The gecko's nose twitched. A little more eye appeared. Not much, but it was all the encouragement Poppy needed. 'It was breathtaking. I almost melted in a puddle at his feet. It was very disconcerting.'

Two eyes now. This gecko was definitely into girl talk. 'I know,' said Poppy solemnly. 'He's going to have to do it again.'

CHAPTER FIVE

SEBASTIAN's day began with a swim and a cup of strong black coffee back at the house. The house stood quiet and empty but for him, and it made him restless, more restless than usual.

Far be it for Seb to admit that he was waiting for Poppy to arrive.

Or that while he waited he turned over in his mind the events of last night.

He'd started it, he knew that much.

He'd finished it too, but only after Poppy had turned to a statue in his arms. If she hadn't stopped, he probably wouldn't have either. They'd have woken together, he'd have brought her some coffee and maybe made love to her again. He'd have made sure they were both sated and satisfied and these next few days could have been made quite pleasurable, and then she'd have gone on her way, no damage done.

That was how it should have played. Could have played.

And hadn't.

Innocence or caution? Or something else entirely? That was the question plaguing Seb this morning, along with another that asked why did he care?

She wasn't his type. Too timid and too plain.

His brother called her mouse.

And then a graceful, slender woman opened his back door without knocking, her toffee-tendrilled hair caught back in a thick ponytail and her cornflower-blue eyes framed by silky brown lashes. Poppy met his gaze and all thoughts, plain or otherwise, fled before Seb's wild and brutal hunger.

'Coffee's hot,' he offered gruffly as she glanced longingly towards the hallway that led to the bat cave. No way. He wasn't letting her off that easily. 'Strong and black with one, right?'

'Right.' She squared her shoulders and headed towards him. 'About last night…'

'What about it?'

'It occurred to me that I may have been sending mixed messages,' she said. 'And I wanted to thank you for your restraint.'

'You're welcome.'

'You're quite the gentleman.' She waved a hand in the direction of Seb's good self. 'Underneath.'

'Underneath what?'

'The recklessness.'

'Poppy,' he said as evenly as he could. 'About those mixed messages. You're still sending them.'

'Oh.' She looked disconcerted. 'Maybe I should just forget the coffee and start in on the work.'

But he'd already poured it for her. He dumped a spoonful of sugar in it and slid it across the counter towards her, spoon and all. 'Take it with you.'

Hospitable, that was him. Gentleman host. As for being reckless…he'd been working on curtailing that particular tendency for quite some time now.

The word *caution* had entered his vocabulary.

Recent lessons involving recklessness and caution had been etched on his soul.

Not so reckless after all, because when she retrieved her coffee with a quick smile and a thank-you and then headed for the hallway, he let her go.

Don't touch. Don't break it. Seb ran a hand through his hair. His hair needed cutting. Work he'd been avoiding needed doing but he made no move towards his office.

Later.

Poppy spent a frustrating day at the computer. Lunch came and went with no Seb to interrupt her. The afternoon rolled by with no progress made when it came to cracking code. Poppy made her way to the kitchen around four. No Seb, but an Esky sat on the bench with a note from him saying that dinner was in it. He made a much better host than she made a house guest. As for flirting and kissing, she had a sinking feeling that he'd decided against continuing along those lines with her.

Hard to blame him, given the mixed messages he'd already chipped her about. Welcome a kiss from him one minute and freeze on him the next? Hide from him all day and then expect him to entertain her the minute she'd gathered enough courage to go and seek him out?

Chances were he wasn't that much of a sucker for punishment.

Poppy took the Esky back to the guest house and put the food in the fridge for later. She stood staring at the ocean for a good five minutes and then, with a curse, she got back on the quad and headed downhill, towards the cove where she'd found Seb yesterday.

Not looking for him, not really.

Good thing, too, because he wasn't there.

Poppy walked from one end of the little crescent beach to the other, and when that did not suffice, she rolled up her trousers and waded up to her knees in the water and watched the black-tipped reef sharks flick about on the outer coral reefs.

Oh, the bravery.

Sick of herself and her timidity and all the risks she *hadn't* taken over the years, she gazed wistfully out over the shallows towards the nearest cluster of underwater coral.

'Coming in?'

Seb's voice, coming from somewhere behind her, and she turned her head and there he was. Board shorts. Snorkel dangling from his hand. Ready to swim. Snorkel. Ready to seize life and wring from it every drop of pleasure that he could.

'No.'

'Shark issues?' He looked towards the outer shallows. 'I'll play spotter for you if you like.'

'Kind of you, but no,' she murmured. 'I didn't bring any bathers.'

'And we're caring about that? You're already half wet. Swim in your clothes.'

Poppy looked towards the closest coral bombie again. It wasn't that far away. Twenty metres? And the water around it looked shallow. 'What's the tide doing?'

'It's on the turn.'

'In or out?'

'In.'

In was good. 'Are there any rips?'

'There's current around the edges of the cove but

nothing serious. C'mon.' He held out his hand. 'You know you want to. I'll keep you company. I'll even lend you my snorkel.'

Poppy smiled faintly. 'What a host.'

'I know,' he murmured and held out his hand. 'You can't come to a sub-tropical island paradise and not swim.'

He didn't know her very well. But the ocean spread out before her, glasslike and beckoning, and several days' worth of unsuccessful code cracking pushed at her from behind, along with her abysmal failure when it came to flirting and kissing with a man who set her aflame.

Surely she could own one small personal victory today? A dip in the ocean. The conquering of a long-held fear. Proof positive that she was making an effort not to be the mouse others believed her to be.

Poppy stepped forward, into deeper water, and found herself up to her waist. Elbows up, the water around that coral outcrop would be deeper than it looked.

And then Seb took her hand in his and coaxed her out further. Neck deep in it now, he turned towards her and smiled. Poppy's fingers tightened around his, not clutching at him but close.

'Where do you want to go?' he asked.

'To the coral,' she said, and tried not to tremble.

'You want me to tow you? Or would you rather swim?'

'Swim.' She could swim. In a pool.

Her heart thudded against her ribcage as she let go of his hand and breaststroked her way towards the coral. Smooth strokes; she *liked* the act of swimming. In a pool.

Seb stayed beside her, matching his speed to hers,

his snorkelling gear looped around his arm. Twenty metres. Twenty metres to the first coral cluster, and she couldn't touch bottom but Seb was there saying, 'Grab my shoulders,' and, 'Now get your head wet,' and then handing her the mask and snorkel. 'Ever snorkelled before?'

'No. I—'

'Let me know if you don't like it, but you have to give it a try. If you stay on the surface you'll be able to breathe normally through the mouth piece. If you dive you'll have to clear the snorkel of water when you surface. You clear it by pushing air through it, short and sharp. That's it. That's all there is to it. I'll hold your waist while you put it on.'

'Seb, I—'

'C'mon, Poppy. In the grand scheme of risk-taking ventures, this isn't one.'

Maybe not for *him*. But she took the mask and snorkel and put it on and that took care of any talking on her part.

'Head in the water, Poppy, while I adjust the angle of the snorkel for you. That's got it. Keep hold of my shoulder if you want to. Grab me whenever you feel the need—I won't mind. And let me show you why I bought this island in the first place.'

The coral came in colours and the colours were green, purple and blue. The fish came in colours too. Bright, daffodil-yellow fish no longer than her finger, black-and-white-striped fish with tiny snub noses. Fish that looked like goldfish, darting in and out of the coral. Silver fish with lilac tails. Poppy jerked her head out of the water, spat the snorkel from her mouth and gasped for air.

'Close, but not quite,' said Seb dryly. 'Now put the snorkel back in and breathe through it—I guarantee you'll get air.' He waited until she had the mouthpiece back in. 'Just close your lips around it. Is it working?'

Poppy nodded.

'Now look again. And this time don't forget to breathe.'

They looked again and this time Seb grabbed her hand and propelled Poppy forward.

He pointed to a rock on the sandy surface, but it was just a rock, not nearly as colourful as the fish. He squeezed her hand and let it go and dived down to touch the rock, only it wasn't a rock at all but a turtle, who went on its way with a grace and offended dignity that made Poppy want to smile.

Seb showed her sea urchins and sea cucumbers, the rolling pattern of clam-lips and the delicacy of orange coral fans.

They went from coral bombie to coral bombie and each one held a secret beauty and the water around it played a clear and vivid blue.

Poppy grew braver in the face of Seb's expert tutelage. She dived down with him and held her breath while they explored. He touched her often and his touch worked magic and when finally they surfaced for a proper breather Poppy didn't realise at first that they were well into the outer waters of the cove.

The moment she did, she was in Seb's arms, clinging limpet-like to whatever sun-bronzed surface she could find.

'I don't suppose this is a thank-you for showing you the reef?' he asked mildly.

'No.' A shudder ripped through her and Seb's arms came around her, holding her close.

'Didn't think so. Have we got a shark problem?'

Who knew? But he was going to have a terrified Poppy problem on his hands very soon if they didn't reach the shore soon. 'It's mostly a Poppy problem at the moment,' she said politely, and increased her stranglehold around his neck.

'Ah.' Thank heaven he remained calm. 'You ready to go back?'

Past ready. Poppy nodded.

'Is distracting you with coral going to work again this time?'

'No.'

'How about kissing you? Dragging you against me?'

'You could, and I'd let you. It's not my biggest problem at the moment.'

'Good to know.' Seb's smile was reassuring rather than predatory. 'C'mon, Ophelia. Loosen up the stronghold and let's get you back to shore. You want a tow or are you going to swim?'

Tempting, so tempting just to say *get me out of here* and leave him to take care of the details, but Poppy could swim, she swam quite well when fear wasn't paralysing her. Lap after lap in friendly gym pools. She could do this.

'Swim,' she said faintly.

'Good girl.' He lifted his hands to her wrists and gently drew her hands from around his neck and put them on his shoulders instead. His hands to her waist after that, sliding down over her bottom and around to her thighs, gentle but firm as he urged her to unwrap her legs from around him too.

He kicked off with an easy side stroke, so smooth and obviously comfortable in the water. Side stroke for him and breaststroke for her, first with one hand on his shoulder and then both hands in the water and her gaze fixed on the shore.

They reached it soon enough and Poppy emerged, dripping wet and trembling, not meeting Seb's gaze until he shoved a towel under her nose and forced the issue.

'Thank you,' she murmured. 'For everything.'

'You swim well, Poppy. Very well. Want to tell me what the panic attack was all about?' he asked quietly, and his eyes weren't condemning, just curious.

Poppy buried her face in the towel and wiped it dry and then handed it back to him. He took it but he didn't use it. Just wrapped it round her shoulders, dripping wet clothes and all.

'I got caught in a rip once when I was a kid,' she began with a shrug. 'My brother too. We got free of it eventually but by then we were a long way out to sea.' She glanced towards the open ocean. Been there, feared it. 'A long way out.'

'Your brother still here?'

'What?' And then it twigged that he thought this story had a tragic ending rather than a happy one. 'Yes. Damon's still here, and unlike me he still loves the ocean. Dares it to swallow him every chance he gets. Me, I've just stayed scared of it. Scared of drowning. Scared of being so tired and disoriented out there that it becomes easier all around to just...' She let a gently sloping hand finish the sentence for her.

'Just what?'

He was going to make her say it.

She'd lain face up in the water that day and felt the call of the deep seep inexorably into her bones. Its siren song and its restfulness; just sink, sink and you'll be fine. You'll be mine.

'Just give up,' she said quietly.

'But you didn't.'

'No. It was a win, I guess. It just didn't feel like one at the time.'

'How old were you?' he murmured.

'Eight. My brother was seven. You'd like him, I suspect. I dare say he'd like you.'

Seb's eyebrows rose a fraction and Poppy summoned a faint smile. 'In a strictly platonic, adrenaline-junkies-of-the-world-unite kind of way.' She glanced towards the water once more. 'I haven't swum in the ocean for years. I guess I could call swimming and snorkelling with you just now another victory. Of sorts.'

Sebastian said nothing, just stood there watching her, with eyes full of shadows.

'Everyone has their demons, Ophelia. Some people never get around to facing them the way you just faced yours.'

'You have demons?' she asked.

'Never doubt it. They're just different from yours, that's all.'

'Will you tell me one of them? A confidence for a confidence in order to make a woman feel a little less exposed?'

He hesitated at first, and then he spoke. 'How do you tell a dead man that you made the wrong call? How do you tell a deaf man you're sorry?'

He was talking about the drill-rig accident, only he hadn't told her about that yet. Mal had. 'There was an accident?'

'An offshore well blowout. My call to send in a crew.'

'But surely there were others involved in that decision? Regulatory bodies. AMSA.' Points to Poppy for remembering names. 'Did your crew have much experience?'

Seb nodded.

'Years and years' worth?'

Another tiny nod.

'Then surely they knew the risks involved and had chosen to take them. Maybe you should factor that somewhere into the guilt equation and see if that changes the balance of things.'

'What if it doesn't?'

'Then ask yourself this. Would any one of your partners, had he been in your position and had he been in possession of the same information you had to hand… Would he have made the same decision to send them in that you made?'

'I don't know.'

'Then I suggest you ask. Alternatively, you could always hole up on a deserted island with a bottle of Scotch.'

'Ouch.'

'I have a missing brother who's off doing God only knows what because he feels guilty that my sister got injured while under his command. For what it's worth, I don't have much sympathy for him either. I did in the beginning. These days I just want to know where he is so I can tell him what a thoughtless, self-centred ass he's being.'

'Again with the ouch.'

'Would you prefer a hug?'

'Yes.' With a gleam in his eye and a tiny smile on his lips. 'Preferably one that doesn't involve you being paralysed with fear for the duration. Think you can manage that?'

'Are we flirting again?'

'You tell me.'

'I don't know. For some people, flirtation comes easy, as easy as breathing. I'm not one of them.'

'You don't say?'

'Doesn't mean I wouldn't like to be better at it. If the opportunity to practise those particular skills ever arose, I'd take it.'

'Practice,' he muttered. 'Whatever happened to meeting someone and just doing whatever feels right?'

'You sound like my brothers. The-fall-in-love-first-and-all-will-reveal-itself spiel is one of their favourites. It's not one they tend to practise, mind, but they're sure it's going to work just fine for me.'

'And it will,' he said, with an endearing touch of desperation.

'But it hasn't,' she countered evenly. 'And at this point in time I am quite okay with the notion of love being an optional extra rather than a necessity. I'd like to learn how to flirt properly, or at least flirt a little better than I do now. And I was wondering...' Dear heaven, she'd been doing more than wondering. 'I was hoping that you wouldn't mind letting me practise.'

'Practise,' he echoed.

'On you,' she clarified. 'Kind of like last night.'

'Poppy, last night was a disaster.'

'Yes, well, I realise I have a long way to go.'

'A long way to—' Seb shook his head as if to clear it. 'What makes you think I can teach you how to flirt?'

'Well, you just helped me conquer one fear. You're an excellent teacher. Patient. Calm. Safe.'

'You're talking about being in the water with me.'

'Yes. You did a brilliant job when it came to helping me conquer my fear. You could do the same when it came to helping me overcome my fear of flirting. Tutor me, so to speak.'

Seb just looked at her.

'I could pay you,' she offered. 'Students pay tutors all the time.'

He stared at her in what looked a lot like horrified fascination. 'Dear God, she thinks I'm a gigolo.'

'Not a gigolo,' she corrected hastily. 'Mentor. There wouldn't have to be sex. We could set boundaries. No sex. Limited touching. Everything in the mind. Just like last night before the kissing started.'

'An emasculated gigolo,' he said and kept right on staring at her in wonder. 'With a masochistic streak.'

'Was that a yes?'

'*No!*'

'Would you like me to give you a little more time to think about it?'

'Again with the *no*. Poppy, at the risk of sounding completely self-centred—which I am—there is *nothing* in this for me besides a headache.'

'What about the joy of teaching?' she said. 'The knowledge that you'd be educating your fellow man, or, in this case, woman? Teach a man to fish and all that?'

'You're serious, aren't you? You really are serious?'

'More like desperate,' she confessed.

'Oh, now, *there's* a compliment,' he muttered, and this time the mortification she'd been holding at bay seared into her, hot and burning.

'No offence intended,' she managed with what little composure she had left. 'I'm not very good with people—you can probably tell that by now. I thought I saw a way to skill up, that's all. And I placed you in the role of teacher because you seemed really good at it. No offence to you intended. None.'

'You're driving me crazy,' he said gruffly. 'You've been here two days and I'm *already* half crazy for even *contemplating* humouring you. Tom'll disown me. Your brothers'll try and kill me. Mankind may never recover if I arm you and let you loose on them.'

They stared at one another in silence until Poppy blushed again and looked away.

'Stop *doing* that,' he muttered.

'Doing what?'

'Blushing. There will be no more blushing on this island. Ever. Got it?'

'Got it,' she said meekly, and blushed again. 'I'm teachable, Sebastian. I know I am. I just need guidance. And that wasn't a blush.'

'Then what was it?'

'Sunburn.'

'I came here to swim,' he said. 'And I'm going to swim. And against all better judgement I will meet you in the billiard room in one hour for your next lesson in male-female relations.'

'Do you mean it?'

He shot her a mutinous look.

'I mean, of course you do. You said it, didn't you? Therefore you meant it. A man of honour is as good as his word. I knew that.'

'God, my head hurts already.'

'Swim,' she said hurriedly. 'Do whatever you came here to do. I'll go and have dinner, have a shower, put on some dry clothes. Is there anything I should bring?'

'If you see my sense of humour anywhere…'

'I'll bring it. I'll bring enough for two. Thank you. Thank you for doing this.'

'Don't thank me yet. You have no idea how wrong this has the potential to go.'

'So we're in a bar,' said Sebastian, and took a hefty swig of his whisky-laced cola. He'd swum, he'd showered, he'd even shaved and put on a white T-shirt to go with the desert island cut-offs that finished somewhere mid calf. He didn't resemble any teacher Poppy had ever known but beggars couldn't be choosers, and, besides, the castaway look really worked for him. She, on the other hand, was showcasing yet another pair of casual beige trousers and a white three-quarter-sleeve boat-neck tee.

'Do we have to be in a bar?' she said as she racked up the balls and rolled them into place. 'Can't we be in a hotel foyer or something?'

'Who's the teacher here?' he said, pinning her with a glittering green gaze.

'You are. No question. Sorry. Continue.'

'So we're in a bar in a hotel foyer,' he said, with exaggerated patience. 'And it's busy.'

'What are you wearing?' she asked.

'Trousers. Collared shirt.'

'Tie?'

'No.'

'Jacket?'

'Too hot.'

'Shoes?'

'Yes, shoes. Not that you care. I am your mentor, not your intended victim.'

'You still look very nice, though,' she said, ignoring the victim crack, and Sebastian sighed hard.

'For what it's worth I'm wearing a sleeveless, A-line, grey-blue mini dress and a pair of black stiletto sandals,' she offered. 'The dress is a little on the conservative side but my soon-to-be sister-in-law was with me when I bought the shoes. The shoes are hot.'

'Is your soon-to-be sister-in-law in on your burning need to become the world's most accomplished flirt as well?'

'No, you're the only one who knows about that particular need.'

'Lucky me,' he muttered, and then, 'How the hell did you get through your teens without learning how to flirt? So you were on the socially inept side, I get that about you. Maybe even the nutty side. I get that too. But look at you. Conservative clothes or not, you're gorgeous. Were the boys around you blind?'

'No, but they were usually a lot older,' she offered by way of explanation. 'I finished school at fourteen and started university at fifteen. I never got to do the high-school social thing. Never did much uni socialising either because I was always so much younger than everyone else.'

They lined up two balls and played for the break. Poppy won it but failed to sink a ball.

Seb studied the table and so did Poppy. Both the nine ball and the twelve ball were on cushions. The coloured balls, on the other hand, were beautifully spread. Not surprisingly, Seb chose to play the coloured balls.

'And when you got older?'

'By then I'd been seconded to a mathematics think tank,' she continued. 'The people there focused on the work and so did I. I worked hard. I didn't get out much. I missed the boat.'

'You hate boats.'

'Which hasn't helped,' she said with a reluctant smile. 'I get out a bit more these days. I'm trying to redress the balance. I go to the ballet. I take a few ballet classes.'

Seb winced.

'I love a good Hollywood revenge movie.'

'Better,' he said.

'I have my plane pilot's licence and I'm working on my helicopter licence. I love to fly.'

Sebastian's eyebrows rose a fraction. 'All right, I'll play that one.' He sank his first ball.

And proceeded to run the table.

'Ouch,' said Poppy. 'That hurt. You could have at least humoured me and dropped a shot.'

'You're a helicopter pilot and a genius. I'm taking my wins wherever I can get them.'

'Fair enough.' They started setting up for another game.

'What else do you do in your down time?' he asked.

'Well, I like to travel. And if Tom and I expand the business and put someone else on—which we're looking into—we can probably both skive a bit more time away from the work. There could be lots of travel. I could go to Cartahegna. There could be treasure maps involved. Riches beyond my wildest imagination. There could be romance.'

'I have no idea what you're talking about,' he said. 'Which does bring me to yet another pertinent question. How do you envisage your impressive IQ fitting in with your seduction plans?'

'Well, it would help if he could keep up.'

'Yeah, good luck with that.' Sebastian's voice was dry, very dry.

'Or I could just not mention it,' she said. 'I usually don't mention it.'

'I pity him already,' said Seb, and played the break and sank a striped ball. But he'd be hard-pressed to run the table this time, decided Poppy.

'So we're in this bar,' he said again. 'You're drinking your beverage of choice. There's a man in a red shirt, shoes, trousers, jacket *and* a tie, and he's been watching you for a while. He's part of a larger mixed group of about a dozen people. The women seem to like him, although none of them are with him. What do you do?'

'I smile at him.'

'He's smiling back. He's raising an eyebrow and looking at me. I don't notice. He's cutting back to you.'

'I shake my head in the negative in the hope that he will interpret this as a signal that you and I are not together. You don't notice that either. You're being particularly inattentive tonight.'

'That's because I'm scoping the blonde in the corner *and* I'm still winning at billiards. I can't be doing everything.' Seb lined up to sink the nine ball…and missed.

'Shame,' said Poppy and opted for the wide-eyed look when Sebastian glared at her. But she couldn't run the table given the spread of the balls either, and, with one ball left to sink, handed the play back to him.

Might as well have conceded the game then and there.

'You gave it your best shot,' he said consolingly, and finished the game. 'Game three, coming up. We need a wager.'

'Not from where I'm standing,' she said.

'Why *are* you still standing next to me?' he said. 'You need to be cutting out from the herd and taking the man in red with you. Take a walk over to the window to admire the view of the pool and the outdoor restaurant. Check out the menu or something. It's sitting there on a stand.'

'All right, I'm going,' she said. 'What do you want to play for?'

'How about who gets to cook dinner tomorrow night?'

'How do you know I can cook?'

'If you can't, you can learn. Isn't that your new motto?'

'Dinner it is. I've just said this to the man in red as well. The odds of this ever playing out in real life are a million to one. I'd have missed every one of my cues, for starters. I'd have smiled at wall art rather than the man and you'd have had to separate me from the herd with a cattle prod. But thank you for the tips.'

The break was Seb's. But after that the game was all hers, and she cleaned up without missing another shot.

'Con artist,' he said. 'New scenario in the here and now.'

'Why does it have to be in the here and now? Why can't we go back to the bar?'

'Because as you've so blithely demonstrated, you are now too comfortable in the bar. You're not feeling the terror of actually presenting yourself as available and willing to explore a connection. It's all in your head.'

There was that.

There was also the small matter of not being able to envision another man worth flirting with when Seb was in the room. Something to do with him being the finest-looking, -sounding and -smelling man she'd ever encountered. And then there were the mind games.

'Fortunately or unfortunately, depending on your point of view, there is a solution.'

'I knew a man of your experience would have a solution,' she said, somewhat warily. 'What is it?'

'From now on you'll be practising directly on me.'

No need to pretend when it came to nervousness—Poppy's had just kicked in, in full.

'And just so we're clear, I'm not a saint, I've never been a flirtation mentor before and I have absolutely no idea where all this might end. Just in case you're still not feeling the terror.'

'I'm feeling it.'

'Not sure you are,' he murmured. 'But you will. Ask me to dance.'

'What?'

'Dance. It involves touch. Touch is part of flirting, and sometimes it can calm a person down and make them focus, like in the water today. And sometimes it can wind a person up. We're going to practise the wind-up variety. Unless you'd rather not?'

'No,' she said, and almost meant it. 'I want to get the hang of this.'

'So.' He inclined his head. 'Anything I should know before we start?'

'Like what?'

'No unpleasant experiences with touch in your past? Something along the lines of the information you could have shared with me this afternoon *before* I took you snorkelling and scared you half to death?'

'Oh.' Poppy offered up a tentative smile. 'There's nothing like that.'

'Because if there is we should stop. That kind of fix is beyond my pay grade.'

'I don't need that kind of fix. I just need practice.'

'Then ask me to dance.' He shot her a crooked grin and picked up his drink. 'I'll be out on the balcony. Whenever you're ready.'

She wouldn't do it. Seb was almost sure she wouldn't follow him outside and ask him to dance. He was calling her bluff. Ending the lesson before it got out of hand. Before he got out of hand and decided that Poppy West was the perfect vehicle of temptation when it came to burying his crisis of confidence and his guilt beneath an avalanche of naked, lust-driven need.

It was dark out here. Nothing but the light from the games room and the stars in the sky to light the way.

Intimate.

She'd never be up for it.

Too wary, and so she should be.

All he had to do now was wait her out and it would be lesson over. He'd go to bed wanting, but his integrity would be intact.

Teach her to flirt. How the hell did a man teach a woman to flirt without taking ruthless advantage of her relative inexperience?

Answer: he didn't.

And then the sliding door opened and Seb stifled a silent groan as Poppy the mouse headed his way.

'Hi,' she said quietly. 'I noticed you were alone and it's a lovely night and there's music playing. Would you like to dance?'

'Oh, that was *good*,' he murmured.

'Really?' Her smile spoke of tentative pleasure. 'I'm winging it.'

Heaven help mankind when she really learned to fly.

She held out her hand and he took it with a suddenly fragile heart. Distraction was one thing. Poppy West was quite another. He'd been a little slow on the uptake in that regard, but realisation was kicking in now and along with it a healthy dose of fear for what might be coming.

Poppy West was vulnerable. And so, right now, was he.

'So,' he said, for he was all for at least *trying* to play his part. 'The trick to dancing with a potential mate is the same trick you've been learning when it comes to conversation. Be attentive and responsive. Make him believe there's nowhere else you'd rather be.'

Poppy smiled.

'Good start,' he muttered. 'Do ballet dancers waltz?'

'They can,' she murmured. But Poppy never had. Not with a man who made her feel like this. 'You still smell like the sea.'

'You smell of cinnamon and ginger.'

'That would be your bath gel.' If this was a waltz, it was a very slow waltz. Seb took his steps in miniature, barely moving, and soon enough both of his hands were at her waist, and hers were on his shoulders. Shades of this afternoon, while swimming in the sea with him, only he was right about there being more than one type of touch. There was the type that soothed. And then there was this. 'What do I do next?'

'Put your arms around my neck.' Nothing but a husky whisper, but she heard him and she did as she was told and revelled in the contact it brought her. The touch of his hair against her fingers and the brush of her breasts against his chest.

There would be no kissing him unless she stood on tiptoe and he bent his head or lifted her up, but there was plenty else to be going on with. The rasp of solidly muscled thighs against her slender ones. The hardness in him and the scorching heat. And then he ran his fingers slowly up and down her spine and almost set her to melting.

She gasped, she couldn't help it, and his eyes took on a slumberous slant. 'Responsive,' he murmured. 'That's good.'

He was responsive too, as she slid her hands down over his chest, lingering just a little as his nipples hardened beneath her palms. Downwards, after that, and more slowly than before as heat coiled in the pit of her stomach and she tried to remember the lesson to hand. 'What do I do?' she whispered when she reached the hem of his T-shirt.

'Whatever you want,' came Seb's low, ragged answer, so she slipped her hands beneath his shirt and put her palms to skin and slid her hands back up his chest. She'd been wanting to do this since the moment they'd first met and finally she had his permission. Even if it was for teaching purposes only.

And then he was hauling his shirt over his head and bringing her back into the circle of his arms and there was very little space between them this time and practically no movement at all beyond Seb's laboured breathing and hers.

'You won't stop me?' She slid the pad of her thumb over the hard nub of his nipple and felt his indrawn breath more than heard it.

'Not yet.' Barely more than a growl. 'Isn't that what you're after? Getting used to a man's touch?'

'Yes.' As she put her lips to the strong column of his neck and felt his big hands slide down over her buttocks and tighten.

She tasted his skin and came away with salt on her tongue. And then she did something else she'd been wanting to do to a man for a very long time and that was set her mouth to his nipple and lave it with her tongue. She grazed him with her teeth and rolled over the nipple again with her tongue and finally she closed her lips around him and sucked.

Things happened in a bit of a blur after that but the end result was effective. Poppy, with her back to the wall and her legs wrapped around Sebastian's waist and her arms tangled around his neck. His lips nudged hers. Not kisses, not quite, but little rubs, this way and that and no tongue whatsoever as she settled to the feel of his erection pressing tightly against her core.

Poppy wanted never to move again but Seb had no such inclination. He rocked against her, into her and she closed her eyes and sought a deeper contact with his mouth.

'Hold still,' he muttered, and then he kissed her again and this time his mouth remained motionless but his tongue did not and his body did not and the feelings he drew from her were wilder and more intense than she'd ever imagined.

And still not nearly enough.

He'd given her permission to do whatever she wanted. She wanted more and took it, deepening the kiss and pressing helplessly against him as he shifted her against him again, positioning her for maximum friction and explosive effect.

Breathing became a hardship. Undulation became a given for the rhythm he set was an irresistible one.

When breathing became impossible, Poppy wrenched her mouth away from Seb's with a gasp and let her head fall back against the wall, eyes half closed as she felt her body begin that final climb.

Too soon. She was rushing him. It wouldn't do to rush him. Not when she still had so very much to learn. Poppy tried to slow down, get her body to relax, but her body had been waiting for a man's touch for a very long time and as for her mind, well…maybe her mind had been waiting for this particular man's touch all along.

Seb's hands were full, but his lips were free and he dragged them across her cheek and down her neck with the delicacy of a connoisseur and every intention of driving her insane.

'Don't stop yet,' she whimpered. 'Please, Seb. Not yet.'

He didn't, just hiked her effortlessly higher and set his lips to her collarbone and she let go of his arms and did what she'd seen him do just moments before, and got rid of her shirt—up and over her head, and it wasn't smoothly done or sexily done, but done all the same and Seb cursed, but he knew what she wanted without being told and slid her bra strap down her arm and swiped his tongue over the puckered nub of her nipple.

And then he feasted.

Not patient and gentle any more but hard and hungry, hot and wet, and Poppy loved it and cried out her pleasure as her body drew tighter. 'Don't stop.'

'Soon,' he muttered, and took to her other breast,

and she threaded her hand through his hair and kept him there. Soon was not yet. Soon could mean practically anything.

By the time Sebastian decided her breasts had had enough, Poppy was boneless and brainless, with not a thought in her head besides the chasing of pleasure. He kissed his way back up to her mouth, and sometimes his lips were teasing and gentle and sometimes he forgot.

She loved it best when he forgot.

Loved it even more when he slid his thumb beneath the waistband of her trousers and then the rest of his hand followed and her button popped and her zipper slid down and his thumb found its way beneath her panties.

'Stop and I'll kill you,' she whispered into his mouth and meant it and he grinned briefly and then bestowed upon her another of those motionless, all-consuming kisses even as his thumb found her clitoris and stroked.

That was all it took.

Her climax came fast and boy did it come hard and she clung to him and came for him and he swore and slid his thumb just the tiniest bit inside her and let her ride it out to the end, his lips in her hair and his voice low and rumbly.

'Guess who forgot to stop?'

CHAPTER SIX

HE'D wanted her responsive, Seb reminded himself with a tortured groan as he withdrew his hand from Poppy's slick heat. Responsive and attentive and she'd told him she was a fast learner—somewhere in his desire-clogged brain he recalled that she learned fast—but he hadn't expected this. Not the abandonment of her response to him, nor the tenderness and care with which he now pulled back.

It was just his hand, no damage done. Nothing she wouldn't have got years ago at a high-school dance or in the back of some college boy's car.

Nothing to worry about as he slid the straps of her bra back in place and ran a rough hand across her back by way of comfort.

She'd buried her face in the curve of his shoulder. He could feel her breath on his skin and what he hoped to God was sweat on her cheeks and not tears. He couldn't do tears. Surely there was no need for tears?

Her chest heaved as she shuddered against him and then slowly she unlocked her legs from around his waist and set her feet to the floor.

Her face, however, remained hidden from his view.

'Hey,' he said as gently as he could. 'Everything okay down there?'

'I'm not blushing,' came the muffled reply.

'Course you're not.'

'And I'm not sorry.'

'I'm glad to hear it.' Not tears, then. Defiance. He liked defiance better. 'I'm thinking no slow dances in public places for you,' he murmured and loosened his hold around her and let her move away. Not all the way away, mind. He still held her in his arms. His body still ached for release but he had himself under control, after a fashion, and there was still a snowball's chance he could convince her that what had happened here tonight was nothing to worry about.

Just a perfectly normal expression of wanton sensuality. Happened all the time.

It hadn't been a revelation at all. Nope.

Say it often enough and he might even begin to believe it.

'Is there anything you'd like me to do for you?' she said, still talking to his chest, and he almost dropped her in his haste to retreat.

'No,' he barked and took two more giant steps back. 'I'm fine.'

A man's self-control would only stretch so far and his was already set to blow.

'Are you sure?' She was staring at his crotch again and when her gaze finally met his there was wry amusement aplenty in it along with a hefty dose of concern. For him. 'You look a little…cramped.'

'I'll get over it,' he muttered. Alone. 'I'm a little low on self-control at the moment, Ophelia. Probably best if you stay right where you are and I take a couple more steps back.'

'*You're* worried about self-control?' she muttered. 'How do you think I feel?'

'Content.' He nodded hard, willing contentment upon her. 'Not in the least bit curious to know anything more about flirting.'

She eyed him steadily enough and then went and spoiled it all by chewing thoughtfully on her lower lip.

'I wouldn't say that,' she said mildly.

'It'd help if you didn't say anything at all,' he offered. 'Here's the thing, Poppy. You lose control and we both have a good time. *I* lose control and you're going to pay.'

'Oh.'

He could almost see the wheels ticking over in that horrifyingly convoluted mind of hers.

'What if I got you drunk?' she said at last. 'I hear that can make a man more inclined to slow down somewhat.'

'Where the *hell* did you hear that?'

'So…it's not true?'

'There are many stages of drunk. Not one of them is going to help me slow down if I get you naked. Lesson's over, Poppy.' He picked up her shirt and handed it to her. Found his and pulled it on. 'And I really don't think I can handle another one.'

Poppy was getting used to driving back to the guest house in the dark and with her emotions in turmoil. She hit the turn too fast and skidded and felt the thrill of it. She went through the unlocked front door without a thought for pirates or critters lying in wait for her inside. She wanted a bath and the music on and set about making it happen.

The bathroom in this place had been a glorious surprise.

Sunken bath with floor-to-ceiling windows on three sides. These windows actually had pull-down blinds attached to them; she'd drawn them down before when bathing but not tonight.

Tonight, she wanted the candles around the bath lit, and the stars shining down on her and a glass of wine by her elbow as she shed her clothes and stepped into the water.

Sensation to replace the memory of Seb's hands on her, and his mouth. Of her mouth on him, and the gentleness in him and the strength. As far as lessons went it had been a doozy. As far as lovemaking was concerned, it had been a revelation.

She wasn't a wanton, never had been before.

And, yes, there was probably an element of pent-up longing for a lover's touch in her response to him. Frustration, even.

But no amount of pent-up longing or frustration had ever driven her to the actions she'd taken on this island. The flirting and the cajoling. The lusting.

The begging.

She reached for the soap gel and began applying it liberally to her arms. Cinnamon and ginger, old-spice and cloves. A masculine scent but she wanted it on her, and she wondered, with the stroke of her fingers along flesh, what Sebastian was doing right now and whether he was showering and what he might be stroking and how hard and how fast, and she closed her eyes and gave herself over to that image very readily, while the water lapped around her and the smell of cinnamon filled the air.

He would give himself over to a shower with the same pleasure he gave himself to the ocean, and the water would stream down his body and find all the valleys as he'd unerringly found hers.

Experience: she wanted it, craved it, but it wasn't *just* a desire to get laid that had Poppy coming apart beneath Sebastian's touch.

It was him.

'Call her back to London,' Seb told his brother the minute Tom answered the phone. He'd lifted weights. He'd had a shower. He had a cunning plan.

'And good morning to you too,' uttered the wise arse cheerfully. 'What's she done now?'

'She's driving me insane. And I think she's a virgin.'

'What?'

'Innocent. Untouched.' Mostly untouched, he amended silently. He still hadn't broken anything. Yet. 'You want a dictionary? And do you *have* to sound just like her?'

'I don't sound anything like her,' said Tomas. 'Clearly you're imagining things. Has she finished her work yet?'

'I don't *know*. How would I know?'

'You seem to know plenty about the state of her hymen,' muttered Tomas. 'Call it a foolish assumption.'

'She's not my type,' said Seb.

'You have a type?'

'Yes, and she's not it!'

'In that case, what's your problem?'

Seb didn't *know* what his problem was. But he did know it started and ended with Poppy West. 'Just call her back to work. Make her leave. That's all I ask.'

'I can't. There's nothing that would make her come

back. Not before she finishes with the code she's running.'

'No one's that work driven.'

'She's not. This job's personal. Poppy needs to finish it. For her sake, and for her brother's.'

Silence from Seb.

'You have no idea what I'm talking about, do you?' asked Tom.

More silence from Seb.

'Would it do any good whatsoever to suggest you at least get to *know* Poppy before you bed her?'

'That's what I told *her*,' he replied curtly. 'Fall in love first, I told her. Not that she *listens*. She does not listen. She's a terrible student.'

This time the silence belonged to Tom. 'Student?' he enquired warily.

'I'm teaching her how to fish.'

'Ah.'

Silence from them both.

'You know, you really could use a break from the island,' said Tom.

That did it.

'Then get your lily arse over here so I can leave!'

'Whatever it is you're doing, it's working,' said Tomas to Poppy on the phone the following morning. 'You can probably stop now.'

'What?' Poppy had just crawled out of the cave in order to answer the phone. Sebastian was nowhere to be seen. He'd been nowhere to be seen all morning. Probably halfway up a cliff face or deep in the belly of a shark by now.

She'd tried telling herself that his prolonged absence

didn't bother her and that it had nothing to do with the events of last night. She'd tried focusing on her work instead. Neither had been very effective.

'Seb's ready and willing to leave the island,' said Tomas, bringing her back to the present with a thud. 'Thanks for the motivational push.'

'It wasn't intentional.'

'I don't care. He's been there too long. He needs to re-engage. How's *your* work going?'

'I'm throwing everything I have at it. Nothing yet.'

'Have you considered that this might be one code you just aren't going to break?' he asked with studied gentleness.

'In a word? No. Failure is not an option. I just need more time.' Poppy ran a hand through her hair and would have paced the room as well had the phone allowed her to. 'As for your brother, if he wants off the island so urgently, can't he just leave me here and go?'

'He won't.'

'I don't need a babysitter, Tomas.'

'It's a little isolated, Poppy. I'm kinda with Seb on this one.'

'And if people *do* insist that I need a carer, there's always the option of asking a friend to come and stay a few days until I'm done. I know plenty of Action-Man types who would happily play hero. All I'd need is your okay to issue the invite.'

'Don't ask me,' muttered Tomas. 'Ask Seb.'

'Well, I would if he were *here*. But I haven't seen him yet today.'

'Where is he?' asked Tomas. 'I'm confused.'

'Aren't we all,' muttered Poppy. 'Was there anything else?'

* * *

The rest of the day passed excruciatingly slowly for Poppy, and it wasn't just because Seb came back around lunch time and started pacing the outer office like an irritated lion. He made calls and took them. Ordered emails sent and paced some more. Man with an almighty need to be somewhere else, decided Poppy grimly, and whether it was due to circumstance or on her account she didn't know.

She doubled her efforts when it came to cracking code. She crashed the bat-cave computer—and the household electrical circuits—twice. And she was still no closer to reading Jared's file—if indeed it even was Jared's file.

Who knew?

'I'd ask you what the hell you're doing,' muttered Seb as he headed out to reset the generator again, only this time he'd decided to take Poppy with him for her future reference. 'Only it's obvious you don't know. Otherwise you'd stop doing it.'

Poppy spared him a cutting glance, which quelled him not one little bit.

'You look like Tinkerbell having a tantrum,' he told her.

'Don't you have some fishing to do, Peter? Lost boys to lead?'

'Fishing's not 'til later,' he said. 'Fresh is best. And the lost boys are making do without me at the moment and apparently doing just fine. How's *your* work going?'

'How do you think it's going?' she snapped.

'That well,' he murmured. 'Anything I can help you with? Besides bringing Gotham City's power grid back online?'

'No,' she said. 'But thank you.' The thank-you was

an afterthought, and he knew it, but he showed her how to reset the power board and crank up the generator, and this time Poppy's thank-you came faster and far more freely.

'I'm sorry,' she said next. 'I'm not making any progress and Tomas phoned this morning and said you wanted off the island. He also said you didn't want to leave me here on my own. I hate the thought of you waiting on me to finish when I don't know how long it's going to take. But I do have a solution. You go. I'll stay. And I'll get someone to come and stay with me.'

'Who?'

'Trig, if he's around. Another one of Jared's friends if he's not. They're very reliable. Ready for anything. Pirates would not get past them.'

'No.'

'Or Lena, my sister.' Probably not a good time to mention Lena's injuries. 'She's at Damon's beach house at the moment. She could be here tomorrow.' Probably.

'Just do your work, Poppy,' he said gruffly. 'Give me an update at the end of each day on how close you are to finishing and I'll plan around it.'

'It's really not that kind of project,' she said awkwardly. 'It'll either come together in an instant or it won't come together at all. There's no halfway.'

'Story of your life,' he muttered, and Poppy blushed on account of last night and because he was right.

'I can be quite singular in my thinking at times, it's true. Sometimes I need reminding about the bigger picture but I am seeing it. I heard what you said last night about not giving me any more lessons, Sebastian. I'm good with that. I understand that having you mentor me was not a good idea. I'd even go so far as to say it was a really bad idea. Still, I've learned a lot and I do thank you for it. Most instructive.' She nodded vigorously. 'Plenty to be going on with.'

'Going on with?'

'Elsewhere,' she said.

He stared at her for what seemed like for ever, his mouth set and his eyes guarded. 'Tom says that if I want to know what you're doing here that's so important, I should ask.'

'Oh.' What to reveal? 'Well, it's, ah…a little convoluted, but the short answer is that I'm trying to find my missing brother.'

'Well, you won't find him here.' Seb's eyes narrowed on her suspiciously. 'Who did you say your brother works for?'

'ASIS.'

'So he's a spook.'

'He really doesn't say.'

'So what do your brother's employers have to say about his disappearance?'

'They say they're looking into it,' said Poppy quietly. 'And so am I.'

Seb sighed heavily. 'The only reassuring thing about that mild-mannered little statement is that you currently don't have internet access. Or do you?'

'No. Internet access is the last thing I want. That's why I'm here.'

'For the privacy,' he murmured. 'Tom says you're one of the best cryptologists in the world.'

'He said that?' asked Poppy. 'That's really sweet. Now if you'll excuse me, I really should get back to the cave. I think one of the cooling fans is glitchy—at least, that's what I hope it is.'

'You're not going to tell me, are you?' He didn't like that. She could see it in the hard glitter of his eyes. 'Trust me with your body but not with your secrets. How does that convoluted brain of yours justify that?'

'Easily,' she said quietly. 'They're not my secrets.'

She wasn't online hacking government systems, decided Seb grimly as he watched her head along the corridor back towards the bat cave. That was a plus. Chances were she'd done that *before* coming to the island. So what was she *doing* here? Reading files? Trying to read files? Government-encrypted files full of classified information and dangerous little secrets that might lead her to her brother? That was Seb's best guess, given the information to hand.

Don't tell her it was illegal or impossible, just give her the tools she needed and stand back.

Seb vacillated between horror at the kind of trouble that would rain down on her if she was caught and admiration that she would dare to attempt such a thing.

The hell with meek and mousy.

Ophelia West had nerves of steel.

He shouldn't be impressed.

So what if he had a few more words to describe her now? Words like *bold. Courageous. Loyal.* And *utterly captivating.* She'd turned his world upside down in a matter of days. Made him ache for her and fear for her and want her more than he'd ever wanted a woman in his life.

His initial reasons for wanting off the island had been noble. Don't seduce the defenceless house guest. Stay away from Tomas's boss.

His reasons for wanting off the island now were a

whole lot more complex, and included leaving before he discovered that she possessed every last quality he'd been looking for in a woman and then some.

Seb spent the rest of the afternoon in the shallows around the island. Ostensibly, he was on a seafood-collection run, but if his eyes scanned the horizon for sign of visitors more often than normal, and if he was on the lookout for any signs of human life on the island, well, blame it on Tom's not-so-law-abiding house guest and a few too many James Bond movies.

Had she managed to make off with government files undetected? Was anyone watching her? Just how important *was* her brother to ASIS and the like? Too many questions and not nearly enough answers, and he made his way back to the house in no better mood than he'd left it, and started in on the cooking with a haphazard-ness the ingredients didn't deserve.

He went to see if Poppy was still working, and she was. Single-minded, she'd said.

She had that right.

He could probably add it to her list of faults.

'You coming out for food or do you want it in here?' he asked from the doorway, and Poppy whirled around at his words, but her mind was elsewhere. He knew that look. His brother wore it often. 'Food,' he said again.

'Yes?'

'I'll bring it in.'

'Oh.' She was still firmly locked in the middle distances. 'I'm almost… I'll just…'

'Keep going,' he said. 'With any luck, you'll have remembered my name by the time I return with your dinner.'

He could add vagueness to her list of faults too. Rack

up a few more irritations and he might even have a snowball's chance of forgetting her and getting on with his life.

'I already remember your name,' she murmured, and just like that her connection to the work was broken and her attention focused entirely on him. 'And your face. And your form. Even *with* a shirt on.' She shrugged and offered him a rueful half smile. 'Have a little faith.'

Flirt.

Seb slid the pile of freshly shucked oysters into the pot of simmering, tomato-based sauce.

Tease.

A pile of scallops went into the mix too.

Fast learner. Very fast learner. No more flirting lessons for Poppy West. She didn't need them.

Feed her, let her do her work, hope to hell she finished it soon and then get her off the island—that was the master plan. She could already hold a man's attention and leave him wanting more and if that wasn't seduction then Seb didn't know what was.

And then the lights went out because the power had cut out again and Seb heard cursing from the direction of the bat cave that would have done a seasoned rigger proud.

He grabbed a torch from the kitchen cupboard and headed for the door. Poppy met him on the way to the generator and one look at her face and any smart-arse comment he might have made died on his lips. Poppy looked shattered, defeated, and his heart went out to her.

'Sorry,' she murmured.

'It happens.' Especially around her.

Her eyes lightened for just an instant and then she

turned back to the power board and started checking switches. 'Can I try and bring us back on, this time?' she asked, and Seb nodded and watched her work through the power board and the generator start-up as if she'd done it a thousand times before.

Maybe she had.

'Feel like taking a break?' he asked gently as they headed back inside.

'Yes. I'll come out and join you for the food. I hadn't forgotten, I just—I'll just start the computer up again first and see what blew,' she said, and he knew it would be useless to argue with her. 'I thought I had it.' She ran a shaky hand through her hair. 'Just before the power went. I really thought I had it.'

'Had what?'

'The key.'

'Key?'

'Code.' She shook her head. 'Please, Seb. Just don't ask.'

He didn't ask.

He went back to the kitchen. He left her alone and went back to the kitchen and it cost him plenty, but he did it for both their sakes, so that Poppy could keep her secrets and he could keep his distance.

Sticking with the master plan, and if he glanced down the hallway far too often in anticipation of her arrival at least no one was there to see him do it.

He'd served up and was about to take the spaghetti to her when finally she arrived.

'Smells good,' she said lightly. 'I need to thank you for feeding me.'

'What blew?' he asked.

'The fan. I swapped it out. The computer's fine. And we can leave tomorrow.'

'We can?' He took in the relaxed set of her shoulders and the sparkle of satisfaction in her eyes. She smiled, and it was the most joyous smile he'd ever seen. 'You did it?'

'I did it.'

'So you know where your brother is?'

'Kind of.'

'So what happens now? You go after him?'

'That's really not part of the plan. The main thing is that we know Jared's alive.' Her voice wobbled precariously on that last word and Sebastian ignored it for all he was worth. 'You have to understand that before now, we didn't even know that. I don't know what happens now. Family conference. Lena will want to make contact with him somehow. Damon'll say to leave him be. Chances are I'll side with Damon.'

'Finally, some common sense. Who'd have guessed?' Sebastian headed for the fridge and the white wine chilling in it. He poured for them both and handed her a glass. 'Here's to your success. May your brother return safely home soon.' He waited a beat. 'Because I'm all for letting *him* tear strips off you for poking around for information in places you shouldn't.'

Rather than answer him, Poppy decided it was time to sample her wine.

'God, you're a piece of work,' he muttered. 'I looked at you before and saw the little girl who almost went under. A timid geek girl with limited real-world experience, only that's not you, is it, Poppy? You know exactly what you're doing—how dangerous the knowledge in your head can be—and you probably always have.

You know all about caution, and courage and choice.
You deal in it every day.'

'I wouldn't say that.'

'You had me completely fooled.'

'Or that,' she said quietly. 'I'm just me. And some
people get that I'm a sum of many parts and some parts
are skilled and knowledgeable and some parts aren't. A
lot of the work I do is confidential. Always has been,
always will be. I don't talk about it. Ever. This latest
job was personal, and I *have* talked about it with you—
probably unwisely. I haven't been cautious at all. As for
courage, I've never had much of that but I'm working
on it. I swam in the ocean. I kissed you and didn't want
to stop. If I'm changing before your eyes it's because I
really am changing—right here and now—and I think
it's for the better. Can't you think *more* of me for fighting my fears rather than less?'

Poppy lapsed into silence and so did Seb. Wine
seemed like a good idea. Filling his mouth with food
seemed like another one. Finally, towards the end
of the meal, he tried sorting his feelings into words
for the benefit of the woman sitting opposite. The one
with the bruised blue eyes who in cracking whatever
code she'd just cracked had probably just accomplished
the impossible. The one who humbled him when it came
to fighting fear.

'I do think more of you,' he admitted gruffly.

He worried for her too. The recklessness with which
she bestowed her kisses. Her next dip in the ocean could
well involve swimming a marathon, and as for her work
and the trouble she could get into there…he didn't want
to think about it.

'I'm happy to leave in the morning,' she said. 'I'll ring Mal. See if he can pick me up.'

'I'll take you. I'm heading off the island too.'

'Thank you.' She looked at him when she spoke this time. 'I've been thinking about how to say sorry to a deaf man. You write him a note. And you stand there and you let him see your face when he reads it.'

'That easy, huh?' he said wryly.

'Yeah.' Her smile came soft and rueful. 'No courage or sorrow or determination to lessen the risks for future oil-rig workers required at all. Nothing to it.'

'Poppy,' he began, and stopped. He didn't know what he wanted from this woman but he did know he wanted more of it. 'I don't know what your plans are, but I'll be staying at a resort in Port Douglas tomorrow night. Would you like to have dinner with me?'

'I'd like that,' she said quietly. 'I could practise my new-found flirting skills on you. We wouldn't be on the island any more. You could be my intended victim as opposed to my mentor. I could stun you with my wit and charm. Dazzle you with my stunning good looks and newly purchased sexy attire.'

She didn't have to dazzle him with the little things; he'd already been blinded by the heart of her. But he summoned up his flirtiest smile and he played the game the way she wanted it played. 'Well, you can try.'

CHAPTER SEVEN

THEY were in a bar. One of those tropical beach resort bars that made heaven look insipid. The swimming and wading pools surrounding it seemed to run for ever and the smell of luxury drifted through the air and seeped into the skin of the people who filled the place.

Money had never been an issue for Poppy. Her family had always had it and her own efforts to accumulate it were not insubstantial. Walk-in room rates had been easily paid. A frock for the evening had been easily paid for too and, though it was not of the calibre of the baby-doll dress and trench coat Ruby had bestowed on her at Christmas, it did have lovely lines and a classy casualness about it that matched the tropical location. The colour was a deep, muted pewter—not her usual pastel fare—and the bodice fitted her closely and the skirt floated around her ankles like sea foam. The shoes were black and strappy and the heels were almost three inches high. The shoes were hot.

The bar was full of confident, beautiful people and Seb was at her side looking more at home and confident than all the rest. Women watched him, their eyes sharply acquisitive.

Men watched him too, some with acquisition in mind and some who just wanted to protect what was theirs.

She'd opened her mouth to make some savvy entertaining remark half a dozen times already, and shut her mouth again without uttering a word. There was a chasm between learning how to flirt with a man and actually doing it and that chasm was never so deep as it was now.

She didn't belong here. Didn't feel comfortable or confident or knowing. Give her an almost deserted island and a tiger shark any day. Give her people who knew about the way she shrank in crowds and didn't care that she wasn't the life of the party and never would be.

Deep breaths in the hope of finding courage from somewhere. A small casual question to answer as Seb asked her what she wanted to drink.

'Whisky,' she said, so he ordered two and she stood beside him wordless, motionless and wishing herself somewhere, anywhere, else.

'Bartender's cute,' he murmured as they waited for their drinks.

The bartender was a woman.

Funny how reality never quite delivered what the imagination could.

'I don't know what to do,' she admitted quietly.

'You could always try and relax. I guarantee it'd help.'

The bartender gave them their drinks. She drained it in one gulp.

'Not like that,' he said dryly. 'I think all this rampant flirting with me's doing your head in. How about we try something easy?'

'Like what?'

'Smile.'

She couldn't even do that.

Seb couldn't fault Poppy's dress sense, her figure or her face. She did gamine beauty to perfection, her presentation was flawless, and it worked on him as it was working on at least half the men in the room.

But her bravado of last night had disappeared completely and Seb was rapidly coming to the conclusion that it wasn't just the mechanics of flirting that Poppy had trouble with.

Gorgeous, brainy, introverted Poppy West just didn't do people.

'Are you hungry?' he murmured. 'I'm hungry. Let's eat.'

Which was how they found themselves in the open-air restaurant out by the lagoon. Linen tablecloths, flickering candlelight, unobtrusive wait staff and a menu dominated by seafood.

Give Poppy something other than people and their interactions to focus on and she relaxed. Billiards or an electrical circuit, a menu and a wine list.

Seb ordered steak, seafood be damned, and this time Poppy smiled.

'See?' he said, pointing a butter-laden knife at her, for he'd been in the process of buttering his crusty fresh bread. Crusty fresh bread being another thing he'd run out of on the island some time ago. 'Smiling's not that hard.'

'Unless it's on request,' she countered, but she smiled again and ordered the barbecued duck and turned her attention back to him once the waiter had gone. 'Tell me about your work,' she said. 'I'm pretty sure it's a standard getting-to-know-you question.'

'What do you want to know?'

'Is it really as Wild West as people imagine?'

'Used to be. Not any more. There's the lure of the strike, if that's what you mean. But the industry's also heavily OH and S regulated nowadays—anything-goes is gone. People look at the offshore rigs and want to know how to get on one. They think good times and easy money, but it takes a particular type of person to keep coming back. It's hard work. Simple mistakes can cost millions, sometimes billions, and they can cost lives. You have to be comfortable with that, and with the ocean and the isolation.'

Seb's crew had been comfortable with that. They'd been proud of their role as troubleshooters and clean-up specialists, even when the work had been dangerous.

Especially when it had been dangerous.

'Do you employ any women?' asked Poppy next.

'In the Darwin office, yes. I've only ever had one as part of a trouble-shooting crew, though. A doctor, and she was fantastic. You don't send a woman out there without unique skills and instant authority. It's just too hard a road. It's hard enough as it is. You going to call me sexist, Poppy?'

'Wasn't planning to,' she murmured. 'Is that an accusation levelled at you often?'

'Not to my face.'

A wine waiter came and took Seb's order, flirting effortlessly with them both as he did so. Poppy watched the man wistfully as he moved on to service another table of guests and repeated the process, easy as breathing.

'Meaningless banter is not your way,' he told her

bluntly. 'Move on. Embrace the introvert. Buy an island.'

'Why *did* you buy an island?' she asked him.

'Retreat,' he said. 'I wanted solitude and I wanted water. It was either that or a boat. Tom convinced me that an island would be better. Turns out he was right. You, however, introvert extraordinaire, didn't like it.'

'Mainly because I thought you didn't want me there,' she replied with that curious mixture of openness and reserve. 'I could have liked it. I *did* like it. The guest house bed was divine and so were the sunrises. I loved the reef and the quad and the walking tracks. I wish I'd had the time to walk the edge of the island all the way round. Take another dip in the shark cove, sharks willing.'

'Adventurous,' he said.

'Not really. You should meet my siblings.'

'Never compare. Especially if you're the one falling short.'

'I'll keep that in mind,' she said with a gamine grin. 'I'll even stop envying the waiter.'

'That'd be a start. Besides, you can always do those things next time you visit the island.'

'Will there be a next time?' she asked.

'Do you want there to be?' he countered.

'Is this where you tell me to get on with seducing you?'

'Wasn't planning to,' he said. 'You do a far better job of it when you're thinking about something else.'

The wine came. Then the meal came. And Poppy West relaxed into the evening. Finding out what made Poppy tick became Sebastian's newest compulsion.

Watching her respond to him, entering into unguarded conversation with him, only made him yearn for more of her subtle wit and warmth. Winning a smile from her became his greatest challenge.

Flirting wasn't her game this evening, it was his and he rewrote the rules as he went along. Forget the easy compliments and find a connection and then another and then another. Take a spoonful of her dessert and let her share his. Fall in thrall to a sensuality Poppy didn't even know she possessed.

'What are your plans for tomorrow?' he asked her.

'Head down the coast to my brother's beach house. See Lena. Phone Damon and my father. Family conference,' she murmured. 'You?'

'Visit a deaf man. Visit a dead man's wife and son.'

'He had a wife and son?'

Seb nodded. 'Bonnie. The kid's name is Cal. He's seven.'

'You going to tell him his father was a hero?'

'He was.'

Poppy smiled. 'What will you say to Bonnie?'

'That I'm sorry. That I've spent the last month going over the events leading up to the explosion in the hope of finding a problem I could fix so that accidents like that one would never happen again.'

'I like it,' she murmured. 'Did you find anything?'

'No. No apparent human error. No indication from the readouts that the well was about to blow. But there's got to be a better way of monitoring unstable wells so that we know what's going on. I want to put it to the company board of directors that we create an R&D division focused on providing just that. Not just mop-up. Prevention.'

'Are you going to tell Bonnie that too?'

'Wasn't planning to.'

'You should. Then she gets to have the memory of a husband who's not just a hero but also a catalyst for change. I think she'd like that.' Poppy shrugged. 'I'd like that.'

'You would? No recriminations? No wishing Cam had been a different kind of man? One who'd chosen a different line of work?'

'Not if I loved him for what he was,' she said in that mild-mannered way of hers that nonetheless cut straight to the heart of things. 'It seems to me that of all people, Bonnie would have known the type of man her husband was. She'd have known that some people simply aren't content unless they're pitting themselves against the odds. Doesn't mean they're not careful. Doesn't mean they want to die. It's just the way they live.'

'You going to count yourself amongst us, Poppy?' he asked. 'Because some of the calculated risks you've been taking with your work lately sure as hell qualify.'

'They do, don't they?' She sounded quietly pleased with herself. 'I've always thought of myself as the careful one. The cautious one. Life in the background. That's what people expect from me. It's what I've always done. Thing is, people change, inside and out, and these days I want more. I want to make love and embrace the experience. Swim naked in the Pacific at midnight and fear nothing. I want to live *one* day as if there's no tomorrow. And then another. And then another. And I might not want to live every day that way but I do want to live some of them like that.'

She took a deep breath. 'Will you make love with me tonight, Sebastian? As if there's no tomorrow?'

The hell she didn't know how to seduce a man.

'Get up,' he said gruffly, and she stood and so did he. They walked towards the exit without touching. Sebastian signed for the meal in silence and tried to remember important things like his suite number and how they might conceivably get there without him hauling her up against him and slaking his hunger for her there and then.

They made it to his rooms, they made it inside and he shut the door behind them. He asked her if she wanted anything to drink and she said water, so he poured her some, and some for himself.

She looked around the room, much as she'd done the first time she'd stepped inside the house on the island. Keeping her thoughts to herself. Not bothering with small talk.

He was a fair way past small talk himself.

'If I wanted to touch you right now,' she asked, 'where might I start?'

'Hands.' His were currently holding up the bench separating living area from bedroom. 'Arms. Chest. Anywhere.'

She walked forward and stood in front of him. Put a hand to his waist and slid the other up his chest. Her eyes were questioning and it took an age before her lips were poised to slide beneath his. 'Like this?' she whispered and touched her lips to his, soft and fleeting. 'You'll let me know if I do something you don't like?' The downward sweep of her lashes as she touched the tip of her tongue to the corner of his lips and then withdrew. She sent him a smile that spoke of woodland things and fairies, shy and curious all at once.

He caught her hand and slid it around his neck. Curved his own hands around the ledge at his back. And gently claimed her mouth.

Poppy knew better this time, what to expect. The taste of him, and the things his lips could do. Like drag gently along hers and plant kisses along her lower lip while she closed her eyes and waited for him to give her more. Fitting his mouth to hers and drinking deeply now, outwardly still but on the inside an erotic mix of warmth and texture and taste.

She didn't know what to do with her hands. She didn't dare voice her moan of boneless pleasure for fear he would take it as protest.

Seb's mouth left hers to trail across her cheek and jaw and play havoc with the skin just behind her ear.

'Why aren't you touching me?' she whispered and he smiled against her skin and bent his head lower to graze her collarbone with lips and teeth.

'Because I'm taking my time,' he murmured and slid his lips lower as Poppy closed her eyes, threaded both hands in his hair and tried to remember how to breathe.

'Sebastian, please.'

'What do you want?'

'Slow and easy,' she whispered with laughter in her voice. 'Only faster.'

'Not this time,' he muttered, but he picked her up and carried her to the bed and settled down on the edge of it, bringing Poppy's knees either side of him and her butt to rest high on his hard thighs.

'Better?' he whispered, with his lips against her neck

and then lower still, to where her collarbone met the silk of her dress. His hands were at her waist now, fingers to her back while his thumbs drew lazy circles upwards towards her breasts.

Poppy's breasts felt heavy and her nipples grew tight as Sebastian continued his leisurely approach from both above and below. Her thighs started trembling and she gave up all pretence of trying not to saddle him with the whole of her weight. Just how long did a man *need* to get to the point?

And then Seb closed his mouth over her pebbled nipple through the fabric of her dress and Poppy gasped and watched as Sebastian pushed her breast up with his hand and flicked his tongue over her before taking another bite, bigger than before.

'My dress,' she whimpered and his hands moved knowingly to the zip at her back, and his lips abandoned her breasts to nibble once more on her jaw.

'It's a very nice dress,' he murmured agreeably.

'I want it off.'

The zip came down and her bra clasp came undone beneath Seb's hands. He started at her shoulders and, with excruciating slowness, bodice and bra parted ways with her body.

'I'm not complaining, really I'm not, but do you think you could hurry it up?' she begged him when he seemed determined to once more kiss a leisurely path to her other breast.

'Honestly, Ophelia,' he murmured against the curve of her breast. 'You need to catch a train?'

But he set his mouth to her nipple after that and her hands went to his head and she arched into that warm and wicked mouth and cried out when he closed his lips around her and sucked.

'Again.'

So he did it again, to a point just shy of pain, and Poppy writhed and trembled and clutched at his head even as he cursed and drew back before rolling her onto her back and putting a calloused hand and hungry lips to her other breast.

Poppy lay there in thrall to the sensation raining down on her body. The heavy weight of his legs across her own, the rasp of his shirt buttons across her stomach, and his mouth, heaven help her, his mouth was moving down her stomach now and taking her silk dress with it.

Poppy clutched the bedspread, her eyes not leaving him as Sebastian slid the dress from her body, and her panties, and her shoes. His shirt came off, and then his mouth came back to hers and when he pulled away she lifted her head and body off the bed, not ready to give up those kisses just yet. Not until she realised where he was going with that kiss, and how it was down her neck and throat and then on to her stomach and lower.

Languid now, as skin met skin he moved down over her body until his chest was nestled between her parted legs. He kissed her stomach and her hip, then slid one arm beneath her thigh and brought that up to meet his marauding lips too.

Feather light now, the touch of his lips and tongue against her skin, as he rocked against her and she rocked back, her skin chasing his mouth the way her lips had done.

He chased her curves down into the crease where leg met hip and Poppy closed her eyes and let him, her chest rising and falling fast and her breathing loud, every part of her focused on his mouth and where it was and the exquisite tension that came of wondering where it might go next.

He got there eventually, and when he did Poppy's eyes shot open before slowly, slowly closing again as he found a rhythm and kept to it.

Her body responded and her breathing grew louder.

She grew boneless beneath his hands and his knowing, caressing mouth. Boneless and gasping until finally he sent her spinning to the stars.

He let her catch her breath. He put his forearm to the bed beside her waist and traced patterns across her lower stomach with lazy fingers. He let her return to earth.

And then he smiled and asked her if she wanted to do it again.

And Poppy said, 'Yes.'

But when he put his thumb to her centre she said, 'No. Not your thumb, Sebastian. That really won't do.' She slid down and put a hand to his trousers, and found the button and then the zip and undid both before pressing down hard on his arousal. 'This.' So hard and huge against her palm. 'This'll do.'

The rest of Seb's clothes came off and the lamp light played over Seb's magnificent frame, the hard stomach and the muscled thighs, his erection proud and jutting. He let her look and he let her wonder about function and fit, and he let her kneel and put her hand to him, and he threw back his head and stared at her through hooded, half-glazed eyes.

'Firmer,' he growled, so she pressed firmer and his hand covered hers as he showed her how he liked to be touched, and that touch was slow and firmer than she'd imagined, and there was more of him than she'd imagined too, as he came down on the bed again and brought her with him.

Condoms. He found one and took care of it.

'Get on top of me,' he ordered gruffly.

So she straddled him and closed her eyes for he was thick and long, and hot and hard, nestling close to where she wanted him, but not in. Not yet.

A question in his eyes, then. A question in hers.

And then she put her palms to the bed, just above his shoulders and bent down to kiss him and he came up on his elbows and deepened the kiss and Poppy's nervousness ran away.

She wanted this. Wanted him, with an intensity bordering on obsession.

Impatient now, as she ground down against him. Gasping, as his teeth grazed her neck.

One of his hands on the globe of her buttock as he sat up even more and positioned her for entry. The cords standing out in Seb's arms and his neck, the blackness of his eyes and the strain on his face. 'I'm not going to move,' he whispered hoarsely and repeated it like a mantra. 'You just…take your time.'

Man was a saint.

She took her time and she took his mouth, and she clung to his shoulders as she tried to make things fit. But her breath caught and it wasn't with pleasure now, and she tore her lips from his and put her forehead to Seb's forehead instead as she looked down to see what the hold-up was.

'Smaller would be better,' she said in a little voice

and he laughed and set his thumb to her and she sank down on him a fraction further.

'Wrong,' he murmured. Nothing but the tip of him inside her and for that she was grateful. He bent his head and caught her nipple in his mouth and sucked.

Soothed her then, with his tongue on her breast and his thumb on her clitoris, lazy circles both, before he took her other breast in his mouth and pushed into her again.

Poppy measured time in millimetres after that, until the pleasure began to build again and her body began to demand more. Seb knew it, too, as he pulled her down onto him and this time he thrust into her in one smooth inexorable movement.

Poppy was no virgin after that.

'Are you all right?' Concern in Seb's voice and in his eyes. He knew what he'd just done.

Poppy nodded, not trusting herself to speak. Or breathe. Or move.

Seb solved that particular dilemma by rolling her smoothly onto her back on the bed, hooking his arm under one of her knees to raise it, and keeping them locked in deep coitus.

'Breathe,' he whispered, so she breathed.

'Kiss me,' he ordered, so she lost herself in the sensuality of his kisses.

'Trust me,' he whispered as his lips teased one corner of her mouth.

And finally she rocked against him and together they began to move.

Time got measured in pleasures after that. The small pleasure to be taken from making him groan as she set her teeth to his shoulder. The ever-increasing pleasure to be found in Seb's possession, until finally she abandoned all inhibition and hooked her legs around his waist, stayed with him as he went to pull away and cried out her release.

Half a dozen savage strokes later, Poppy came again and this time Seb came with her.

He carried her to the shower some time later and stood them both beneath it. Modesty had no hold on him, and Poppy took her cue from that and let him wash her with gentle hands, and the soap made sliding easy, and his smile made smiling easy.

'Was it what you expected?' he rumbled as she turned the soap on him.

'Better,' she countered and felt a rush of satisfaction as his nipples hardened beneath her hands. 'Best lover I've ever had.'

'I'm so flattered. You think I don't realise I'm also the first lover you've ever had?'

Satisfaction in his voice, laced with a hint of concern.

'I'm not even going to ask what kind of lover I made,' she continued. 'I'm a learner lover. I get points for trying. I hear finesse comes later.'

'You do okay.'

'Actually, I did very little. For example, I barely touched you.' She ran her hands down his arms slowly, to his wrists and back, learning him now, because she'd been too preoccupied to do so before, and he leaned back against the shower-stall wall and let her. 'That's got to be a mistake, hasn't it?'

'Under those circumstances, no.'

'What about *these* circumstances?'

'Depends what you're after.'

'More,' she murmured. 'We're not done here yet. Are we?'

He looked at her, saying nothing. And then he leaned forward and kissed her and his hunger answered for him.

CHAPTER EIGHT

POPPY had spent the past few days on the island waking with the dawn, but the curtains in the hotel room blocked all light and the clock showed eight-thirty when finally she opened her eyes. She sat up slowly and looked around, bringing the sheet with her in an act of belated modesty that no one was around to witness.

The sheet fell to her waist. 'Seb?'

No Seb.

She got up and reached for the hotel robe she'd discovered after her shower last night. She did a quick scan of all bench and table tops in view.

No note.

Seb's overnight bag was still sitting on the luggage rack beside the wardrobe, though, and a black men's toiletries case was in the bathroom, so presumably he planned to return to the room.

After all, it was his room.

Was she supposed to be gone by then? Poppy put her hand to her hair and tried to think through her options. She had no idea of the protocols involved in morning afters. Especially when the night before had been one long and leisurely exercise in education of the flesh.

Wait, people had told her.

Wait until your emotions are engaged. Well, she'd waited, and they had been and Seb had been patient with her, and very tender. Altogether mindful of her pleasure.

Maybe a little bit *too* mindful, for he hadn't lost control with her during the night. Not once had she glimpsed the rawness in him that she'd felt two nights ago out on the balcony. There'd been pleasure for him, of that she was fairly certain. There had been need. Just not the all-consuming, 'I don't even know where I am' need that she'd felt for him.

It was this last point that made Poppy's decision to return to her room easier.

Give the man some space; he obviously had need of it or else he would be here.

Heading for my room then breakfast, she wrote on the hotel notepaper just in case she was wrong. And then she slipped last night's clothes back on and made her way back to her room, and if other hotel guests saw her and labelled it a walk of shame, well, that was not Poppy's take on it.

She'd wanted this, wanted Seb and there was no shame at all in that.

The only pressing concern she had this morning was how Seb might be feeling and how—should he be feeling just fine—she could conceivably ask for more.

Sebastian Reyne was restless. He'd gone down to the marina and the boat this morning to check on the moorings that had been twice checked last night. He'd gone down there because he'd needed the walk and because he'd wanted to clear his head when it came to what had happened last night.

And to try and figure out what to do with Poppy West now.

She'd wanted experience and he'd had it to spare.

She'd asked for one night and he'd given it to her, hadn't he?

And he'd held himself in check and he'd made it good for her. He'd made sure Poppy's first time had been worth the wait.

But some time during the early hours of the morning, between one caress and the next, he'd realised that he wanted more time with this woman. More nights with her, only wilder. More days like the ones they'd already shared.

And he didn't know if that was on Poppy's agenda at all. Hard to tell if she even *had* an agenda beyond facing her fears, seizing the opportunities a moment might bring and being on her way.

He found her in the breakfast atrium, seated at a table for two by a window that overlooked the lagoon. There had been no overnight change to her looks or her wardrobe. Nothing at all to signify that she was now a sexually experienced woman of the world. Her clothes were still on the conservative side, her demeanour just that little bit reserved.

She met his gaze with a guarded one of her own and whatever it was that she saw in his eyes it caused her to blush and drop her gaze. Seb smiled as he eased into the seat opposite her.

Well, well, well.

Maybe the analytically inclined Ophelia West hadn't given much thought to her endgame after all.

'What's good?' he asked, nodding towards her almost empty plate.

'The eggs Benedict and bacon's not bad. Watermelon's good. *And* they have dragon fruit.' She put down her knife and fork and reached for her tea. 'You forgot to leave a morning-after manual.'

'Do you need one?'

'Wouldn't hurt.'

'Sometimes you've just got to go with your instincts,' he murmured. 'This morning, for example, I'm probably going to ask you how quickly you need to get to your brother's beach house and how long you plan to stay there and where you might conceivably be going after that.'

'And you're asking this because...?'

'I'm curious.'

Seb leaned back in his seat, trying to decide just how at her disposal he wanted to place himself. Blushes aside, she hadn't touched him this morning, hadn't solicited his touch in any way. Maybe she did need a morning-after hint or two when it came to making a man feel wanted. And maybe she was following her instincts, as directed.

'I do need to get this new information about Jared back to my family. Especially Lena, who's currently at the beach house. There's a heated pool there. She uses it for physio.'

'Physio?'

'Lena got gut shot eight months ago. A bullet nicked her spine and messed up her ability to use her legs for a while. She's walking again and hoping for a full recovery. She's making remarkable progress.' Sorrow clouded Poppy's eyes. 'Everyone says so.'

'But?' he asked softly.

'But I'm not sure she'll ever have the level of physical fitness she once enjoyed. I'm not sure she's admitted that to herself yet. She still talks about getting her old job back. It seems a little unlikely.'

'What's the job?'

'Special intelligence recon. Same as Jared. Same as Trig. They were all in East Timor together, checking out an abandoned factory, when she got shot. Lena says they were ambushed. Jared didn't say much at all. He was the one in charge of the recon. He took Lena's injuries hard.'

'I can imagine.'

'He holds himself responsible.'

'I can imagine that too.'

Poppy smiled a little ruefully. 'I'm sure you can.'

'Is that where he's gone?' asked Seb. 'To right a wrong? Is that why you're so worried about him?'

'Maybe.' She shrugged, still not inclined to trust him with other people's secrets, no matter what liberties he'd taken with her body the night before. He could understand her reasoning. Didn't mean he had to like it.

He still hadn't touched her yet. Time to rectify that.

Seb stood and stopped by her chair, one hand on its back and one on the table as he bent down and kissed her lips, lightly at first, and then a whole lot more thoroughly as he met with eager response. 'Want another coffee?'

'Thank you for last night,' she murmured. 'And no, thank you to the coffee, but yes to another slice of watermelon.'

Seb ordered his coffee and filled up a plate from

the smorgasbord selection. He added watermelon and headed back to Poppy.

'So what are *your* plans for the next few days?' she asked lightly.

'Make arrangements to visit Bonnie,' he said, for he'd put it off too long. 'Get that sorted.'

'Bonnie lives in Darwin?'

Seb nodded. 'Then I need to put in an appearance at work before Wendy resigns. Again. It could be some time before I manage to clear the backlog. Ever been to Darwin?'

'No.'

'Want to?'

'Are you asking me to come with you?'

'Not directly. It's more of a fishing expedition. I want to see if the idea has any appeal whatsoever before I commit to an actual invitation.'

'Oh,' she murmured. 'Smooth.'

'Yeah. You probably want to find yourself another mentor when it comes to morning afters. Trust me. I won't be offended.'

'I like the sound of visiting you and seeing you again,' she said, and picked up her tea cup with slender fingers. 'It doesn't really matter where.' She regarded him with a hint of a smile in her eyes. 'Should I have been more elusive?'

'Blunt is good.'

'Good. I'm trying to think of a place that we could both get to with relative ease. Me from Oxford and you from Darwin. How do you feel about Dubai?'

'Unenthusiastic.'

'Singapore or Hong Kong?'

'Same.'

'Why?'

'Maybe I'd rather see you in your working environment. Your normal living environment. Maybe I want you to see me in mine. See if you're interested in me for anything besides the sex.'

'You're feeling used?' Poppy couldn't quite hide her dismay. 'I told you I needed a manual. You need to look at this from my point of view, Sebastian. I practically begged you to have sex with me. For all I know, I'm nothing more to you than a pity—'

'Don't,' said Seb gruffly. 'You're not.'

'I needed to give you an out.'

'Consider it given. And ignored.'

Poppy eyed him uncertainly. 'You're very welcome to join me at the beach house some time over these next few days if it happens to fit in with your plans. And you'd be welcome to visit me in Oxford, once I get back there. Stay with me or stay with Tomas. I can't say as I plan to discuss bedding you with Tomas but I certainly don't plan to deny that we have an ongoing association if it turns out we do.'

Association.

Non-committal word. Maybe she hadn't been as enamoured of their lovemaking as he'd thought. 'Did you have a good time last night?'

'Yes. But then, you made very certain of that. Too blunt?'

'No.'

'Did *you* have a good time?' she asked.

She seriously had no idea what she'd brought to their lovemaking. The joy of discovery. Unselfconscious abandon. Delight. In him. 'I had a good time.'

'Because it seemed to me that you might have been holding back a little. At times.'

He leaned forward and placed the watermelon on her plate. 'Don't complain.'

'It was more of an observation.'

'But not one you need to worry about. Eat your watermelon.'

She sent him a level glance, one he returned in full. She picked up the watermelon and studied it before testing the edge of it with her teeth. 'I'm getting the impression you like to be in control,' she said.

'I'm getting the impression you do too.'

'I don't know where you're getting that impression from.'

Sebastian smiled. 'Call it a hunch.'

In the end they parted company just on midday, with Poppy's flight south leaving twenty minutes before Seb's flight to Darwin. They travelled to the airport together, checked in together and went through Security and into the holding area together too.

Being seen as with someone was a pleasure that was new to Poppy.

Touching Seb in public was a happy new pleasure for her as well. She didn't overdo it; at least, she *hoped* she didn't overdo it. But when a touch to his forearm brought her a smile from Seb and an envious glance from the barista at the coffee counter, it was tempting to turn towards him, rather than away, and let her chest brush his as she turned to check the departure board.

That was what people did at airports. Checked departure boards and drank coffee until it was time to go.

They'd exchanged contact details and she'd given him Damon's beach house address, just in case. 'Are you worried about what you're going to say to Bonnie?' she asked as the minutes ticked away.

'Little bit,' he admitted gruffly. 'Got any advice?'

'None that's backed up by experience,' she said. 'My mother died when Damon was born but that was a long time ago now. Let Bonnie talk if she wants to talk. Take someone else with you if you think it'll help. That's it. That's all I've got by way of advice.'

Seb leaned forward with his elbows on his knees and his head bowed. 'It's as good as any.' He shot her a sideways glance. 'I've got a photo of Cam. Someone took it the day before he died. Hard hat on, manhandling pipe, covered in slick and grinning like a loon. Should I give it to her?'

'Yes,' said Poppy and blinked sudden tears from her eyes. 'I think she'd like that.'

Poppy made it to the beach house just on dusk, to find not just Lena in residence but Trig as well. Separate bedrooms—Lena had been quick to point that out, never mind that it had taken less than five minutes in their combined company to figure that out. Trig prowled about, caught between wanting to coddle Lena and Lena having none of it. Frustration radiated from him in waves to mix with Lena's irritation. Volatility ruled here, not sense. Which made sharing her news of Jared's activities an unwelcome task.

'You look different,' Lena said suspiciously as she thrust a tall glass of soda water in Poppy's direction. 'Trig, does Poppy look different to you?'

Trig looked, his warm brown gaze narrowing as he gave Poppy the once-over. 'Nope.'

'Must you disagree with everything I say?' snapped Lena.

'You asked me a question. I answered it honestly. Bite me,' he muttered, but he turned and surveyed Poppy once more, at which point she lifted her chin and willed herself not to blush. No way could a person take one look at her and determine that Poppy was no longer a virgin. No one was *that* observant.

'No,' he said again. 'Still not seeing it. She's still an absolute sweetheart, the way I see it. Haircut? Colour? New lipstick? What else do men get into trouble for not seeing?'

'The error of their ways,' said Poppy dryly. 'I want to ring Damon but I don't know how private a phone call is.'

'Not private,' said Lena and Trig in unison.

'I cracked Jared's file,' said Poppy, and suddenly found herself in the receipt of Lena and Trig's absolute attention. 'There were barely any details. Jared's employee number. An initial location—the Blue Mosque in Istanbul. A list of half a dozen dates—the last date being five weeks, six days ago. And at the top of the file there seemed to be some sort of title name or level of authorisation or job name or something. I don't know what it meant. It was just one word. *Sentinel.*'

'Never heard of it,' said Lena. 'Trig?'

Trig shook his head, but Poppy had the advantage over Lena in that Poppy had been looking at Trig as she'd relayed the information. She'd seen the flash of recognition in Trig's eyes upon hearing the word *Sentinel.* She'd seen it in his momentary stillness and she would quiz him about it later, make no mistake, but for now, in front of Lena, Poppy was content to follow Trig's play.

'Anyway, I think it shows pretty clearly that *someone* in ASIS knows where Jared is and what he's doing. You said you walked into a trap, back in East Timor. You said they knew you were coming. Maybe there's a leak inside ASIS and Jared's working his way back to it at someone's behest. Maybe there's no reported information in the file because he's working outside of regular reportable channels.'

'Maybe you're looking in the wrong file,' said Lena.

'Damon found it,' countered Poppy quietly. 'It's *all* he found. *You* want to tell him he doesn't know what he's doing?'

Lena scowled her discontent, but Poppy knew she'd made her point. Damon was a hacker, employed by governments and those who monitored governments. If Damon couldn't get to a piece of information, no one could.

'Well, if Jared is working dark point there's *no* point trying to find him,' said Trig.

'You don't know that,' said Lena stubbornly. 'If he's on his own with minimal backup he might need us more than ever.'

'That or we blow his cover to hell and back and endanger all concerned,' said Trig.

'That's always been a concern,' said Lena. 'Didn't stop you from heading off to look for him before.'

'Because we had absolutely no information to go on, before. Now we do. And it's worth asking ourselves if we simply need to stop worrying, step back, and let Jared do his job.'

'I'm with Trig on this one, Lena,' said Poppy mildly. 'The file contained good news, rather than bad. I don't think we need to go looking for him either.'

'And what do you know about it, Poppy? Where's *your* covert operations experience that you can so blithely make such a judgement?'

Poppy took the jab in silence and watched as Lena turned and made her way slowly, awkwardly towards the central atrium and out the already open glass doors, past the pool and into the gardens beyond.

Trig sighed heavily and ran a hand through his short brown hair. 'She doesn't mean it,' he muttered.

'I know.'

'She's torn a muscle in her right leg. The physio told her not to push herself beyond the point of pain, but you know Lena. Now she's banned from doing any stretching exercises at all. The physio threatened hospitalisation and bed rest if Lena continues to work out.'

'Oh.' Poppy offered Trig a sympathetic grimace. 'Happy times.'

Trig allowed himself to look tragic. Byron had nothing on this one when Trig chose to pile it on.

'May I make a suggestion?' asked Poppy.

'Please do,' said Trig. 'Save me.'

'Go away,' she said gently. 'Stay away. Lena pushes herself harder when you're around. She always has. And whether it's because she wants to beat you or impress you, I don't know—I doubt she knows—but until you leave, Lena won't truly allow herself to listen to her body and rest. Besides, you know more about Sentinel than you're letting on. You're going to want to follow that up. No time like the present.'

'You're as bad as your sister.'

'Why, thank you, Adrian,' murmured Poppy, for that was his real name, even if the only people who ever used it were Poppy and his mother. 'You flatter me.'

'Give me a couple of days to arrange a few details and I'll go,' he said. 'But only because I have things to do. Not because you think your sister will rest easier if I'm not around. That's insane.'

'If you say so,' murmured Poppy. 'Who's cooking, tonight?'

'You are,' said Trig.

Lena walked to the water and came back and walked up to Poppy and hugged her in silence.

'I'm sorry, Poppy. I'm so frustrated about not being able to do anything, my temper's set to fire at the slightest pull. I'm driving Trig nuts. I'm already nuts.'

'Only a little.' Poppy continued with the dinner preparation, a stir-fry with lots of vegetables and leftover chicken she'd found in the fridge. 'Hey, wine waiter,' she called to Trig. 'Fill us up.' And he came in and played the fool when it came to pre-tasting it until even Lena smiled. Trig took himself off to Damon's office after dinner, and though Lena watched him go with a frown she made no move to stop him.

'Probably wants us to have a little sister-to-sister time together,' murmured Poppy. 'He's really quite considerate like that.'

'So what was Tomas's island like?'

'Beautiful. Isolated.'

'And Tomas's brother?'

'Sebastian,' said Poppy.

'How was he?'

Poppy nodded and practically swallowed her wine glass whole. 'He was good.'

Bonnie looked thinner than Seb remembered her. More gaunt in the face but her smile was still welcoming as she ushered him inside the house and through to her cheerful, messy kitchen.

'Cal's out in the yard with a friend,' she said. 'They're camping out tonight in a tent in the back yard. There's a campfire and everything.'

Seb headed for the sliding door that led to the yard. 'Looks more like a bonfire.'

'Yeah, well.' Bonnie shrugged. 'Boys. Hey, Cal!' she said at volume before Seb could stop her. 'Seb's here.'

And then Seb's arms were full of small, grubby boy and then of course he had to meet Cal's fellow camper, Dek, and check out the tent and the shower facilities—namely the garden hose hanging from the clothes line—and the campfire and the potatoes wrapped in foil, just waiting to be cooked. Seven years old and lost in play and Cal's words that went, 'This is my dad's best friend,' didn't cut so deeply after that.

Back to the back steps where Bonnie stood watching, and if Seb's gaze was full of silent sorrow she made no mention of it, just made her way back inside. Holding up okay, he decided.

'You right for money?' he asked gruffly as she handed him a beer and poured a glass of wine for herself. 'The policy money came through?'

'It's coming,' she murmured. 'And it's more generous than I ever imagined. I'm set for life now. Cal too. You did good.'

'It's company policy.'

'It's your company.'

'Not just mine. Cam's stake will roll through to you too. It's worth a bit in dividends. Plenty more if you decide to sell the shares outright.'

'I won't be selling them,' she said. 'Cam believed in that company, in the work you do. And so do I.'

Seb had nothing to say to that; his throat had closed up too tight. *Don't talk about Cam.* Maybe Bonnie could but he couldn't. Not yet. He took a swig of beer. 'We're setting up an R&D division of the company. If there's a better way to monitor drill rigs for instability, we'll find it.'

'Go, you,' she murmured. 'I like it. So what else have you been doing besides deciding to change the world?'

Seb shrugged. 'Well, I met a woman.'

Bonnie had smiley eyes. 'You meet a lot of women, cowboy.'

'One that matters.'

Wide, smiley eyes and a smile on her lips to match. 'What's she like?'

'Smart. Shy. I keep waiting for her to run.'

'Why would she run?'

'Risky, loving an oil-man.'

'Risky loving anyone,' countered Bonnie. 'I figure it for the ultimate act of bravery.'

'Do you ever regret it?' he asked gruffly. 'Hooking up with Cam?'

'It's not always easy. You lot live hard. Die young. Isn't that how the saying goes?'

Seb shrugged.

'Still…' she murmured. 'My Cameron knew how to love hard too. All in, and we had some good times. The best times. How can I ever regret that?'

'I told her about you,' said Seb. 'I asked her if I should give you this.' He reached into his jacket and pulled out the photo of Cam and handed it to Bonnie. 'She said yes.'

Bonnie took the photo. Damned if she could see it, thought Seb, what with the tears that started falling, but she nodded and thanked him and the pad of her thumb kept rolling gently over Cam's face.

'Thank you,' said Bonnie raggedly. 'I'll put it on the fridge. Cal's going to love it.' More tears flowed.

'I should go,' said Seb.

'Yeah,' said Bonnie. 'Unless you'd rather sit here and watch me cry.'

'No.'

She laughed at that and wiped at her tears. 'I like your new woman. I like the advice she gave you and now I'm going to give you some. Love isn't always wise, Sebastian. So love as you will and try never to regret it. Your girl understands that.'

Bonnie's thumb slid gently over Cam's face again. 'If she's given you her heart, she's not going to run.'

Sebastian didn't know what had possessed him to head for the airport the moment he left Bonnie's. He'd told Wendy he'd be back at work today. He'd already spent half the morning there. He knew damn well people were wanting his opinion on a number of projects, but he had the work on his computer now, and he was back online and within email reach. Poppy had been maddeningly elusive about whether she would visit him or not, and he needed to see her again before she went back to Oxford. It was as simple as that.

He hired a car from Brisbane airport and drove his

way down the coast to a beach house he had directions to. He didn't think to phone until he'd pulled up in the drive and by then it was too late. He rang the doorbell and waited impatiently for Poppy to answer it, at which point he would say…something clever, only he didn't know what. He rang the bell again and this time the door opened and a slim, dark-haired woman regarded him with what looked like a hefty dose of impatience of her own.

'You'd better not be selling vacuum cleaners,' she said.

'You must be Lena,' he said. 'Is Poppy in?'

'You want Poppy. My sister.'

Blunt was good. He was guessing it ran in the family. 'Yes.'

'And you would be?'

'Waiting to see if you're going to let me in.'

'Not without a name, pal.'

'Sebastian Reyne.'

'Tomas's brother?'

'Yeah. Tom's brother.' Good ole Tom's brother. Poppy hadn't mentioned Seb to her sister. It didn't bode well for an enthusiastic greeting but he stood his ground, for he'd know soon enough.

Lena stepped back slowly, carefully, and Seb finally got around to noticing Lena's pallor and her white-knuckled grip on the door. 'You all right?'

'Don't you start,' she muttered. 'I pinged a muscle or something on the way to the door. It's nothing. Not even worth mentioning. To anyone.'

The door opened wider. 'The kiddies are playing in the pool.' Lena looked back over her shoulder as Seb stepped inside. 'No, Poppy's out now.'

The beach house had been built around a central open-air entertainment area, complete with roof and pool. The engineer in him wanted to linger over the design but Ophelia was indeed out of the pool, wearing a yellow and red polka-dot bikini her soon-to-be sister-in-law had probably bought for her and dripping water all over the tiles.

She wasn't alone. A bulked-up, bronzed Adonis hauled himself out of the water to stand beside her, smiling with easy familiarity as he responded to something she said. The man grabbed a couple of towels from a nearby pile and handed one to Poppy. Poppy did not look at all uncomfortable about being nearly naked in front of this man and she sure as hell didn't appear to be having any trouble communicating with him.

Possessiveness roared within Seb, but he held it in check.

Could be one of her brothers. Damon, whose house this was, or Jared, freshly back from wherever. Could be that the compelling urge to go over there and stare down the other man and then brand Poppy with his kiss was all kinds of wrong.

He had no problem when it came to branding her with his eyes, though. No problem at all.

'Well, colour me intrigued,' murmured Lena, and in a voice that would carry, 'Poppy, you have a visitor.'

Poppy turned and saw him, her eyes widening. 'Seb!'

The unknown Adonis turned towards him too and then for some unknown reason stepped closer to Poppy rather than away. And then the Big A put his towel around Poppy's shoulders, for she was still strangling hers with her hands, and after that Seb had very little in mind but murder.

Poppy smiled in greeting but her eyes showed no little concern as she headed towards him. 'Is everything okay?'

'I don't know,' he said as she came to a halt in front of him. Seb's gaze cut to the other man now heading their way as he returned Seb's quietly murderous gaze measure for measure. 'Is it?'

'I, ah—' Poppy looked bewildered.

'Introduce them,' murmured Lena. 'That might help.'

'Oh,' said Poppy and blushed.

'About that difference,' the Adonis said to Lena. '*Now* I'm seeing it.'

'Aren't we all,' said Lena.

'Seb.' Poppy's hand went to his forearm and her blush deepened fetchingly. 'This is my sister, Lena, and our family friend, Adrian.'

The name did not fit the man. Good ole family friend Adrian had far more menace in him than that. Adrian offered his hand. Seb took it, shook it, and returned the expected crusher-grip with one of his own. The handshake didn't *look* like a test of strength, but it was. And Seb had the edge.

'Call me Adrian and I'll be forced to deck you,' offered Adrian pleasantly.

'Feel free to try.' Seb's voice was equally pleasant as he released his grip on the other man's hand.

'A little more information, Pop,' muttered Lena.

'Adrian is otherwise known as Trig,' continued Poppy hurriedly. 'Trig for trigger happy. I may have mentioned him. Could have been when we were talking about Marlin fishing.'

Seb let himself relax slightly beneath Poppy's delicate touch but his eyes didn't leave the other man's face.

'Trig. Lena.' A thread of steel had entered Poppy's warm, melodic voice. 'This is Sebastian Reyne, my co-worker's brother. I've been staying on his island. Seb's company troubleshoots offshore oil wells. He's also my, ah…' It was here that the thread of steel began to dissipate. 'My, ah…' Poppy turned to Seb. 'The protocol for this situation escapes me. What are you?'

Sebastian watched as Trig caught Lena's bemused gaze and wicked humour ran thick and swift between them. Only then did Seb allow himself to relax a little more and turn to the stammering Ophelia and raise an enquiring eyebrow.

'Ladies' call,' he murmured.

'Oh, I think we get the point,' said Lena smoothly.

'Damn, Pop. I thought you were saving yourself for me,' teased Trig.

'She probably got tired of waiting for you to grow up,' countered Lena. 'Help me back to the kitchen, would you, please, Trig? I think I pulled that muscle in my leg again.'

Trig paled. Moments later Lena was in his arms and they were heading for the square of sofas in the middle of the big open room, with Trig berating her every step of the way.

Lena looked back at them over Trig's shoulder and winked.

'So has she hurt her leg or not?' murmured Seb. For the life of him, he couldn't tell.

'She's hurt it,' replied Poppy as she watched them go. 'She's trying to hide how much. Lena would *never* show that kind of weakness in front of Trig if she wasn't in serious pain, and Trig knows it. I'll make her a cup of tea. Trig can have a Valium. What'll you have?'

You, he thought as he captured her lips and gave in to the need that had been riding him for what felt like days.

Poppy dropped the towel she'd been holding as Seb hauled her against him. Her arms came up to twine around his neck and the towel fell from her shoulders as she lost herself in his arms and promptly set him on a path he'd never been down before either.

Welcome and celebration. She might have botched the words of welcome but her kiss made him feel savoured and it made him feel cherished.

'Hi,' she whispered as he let her go, mindful of their potential audience and fully aware that it wouldn't take much and he'd have her up against a wall in the nearest empty room or corridor.

His need to possess her hadn't dimmed with their days apart. If anything, it had grown.

'Hi,' he murmured back and felt like a schoolboy again.

She smiled and led him to the kitchen, located on the south side of that central open living area. 'This is a beautiful home.'

'It is, isn't it? Damon found it and bought it but it's fairly safe to say we all love it.'

'What does your brother do for a living?' asked Seb, for it was very clear that the absent Damon did not lack for money.

'He's into computers.' Poppy filled the kettle and set it to heating.

'Like you.'

'Like me, but with a few key differences in approach.'

'You can be very evasive when you talk about your family.'

'Habit,' she said. 'My father's fairly easy to talk about. He works the money market in Hong Kong. What else would you like to know? I can give you the fastest rundown in the West if you like? We've all had pretty good educations. There's no shortage of brains. All of our occupations come with mile-long confidentiality clauses. I think we like it that way.'

'Is *anyone* around here normal?' asked Seb.

'I like to think we're very normal,' she said, and really did pull out a tray of medications, as if getting ready to offer Valium to the beleaguered Trig. 'Even if it's not altogether true. Lena, do you want a painkiller?' she asked at slightly louder volume than the one she'd used on him.

'Bring two,' came the thready reply.

'I'll be right back.' Filling a glass with water from the tap, Poppy took the tray of medications over to where Lena and Trig were sitting. When she came back she was smiling ever so slightly. 'They're going to the hospital.'

'So why are you smiling?'

'Because it's about time. According to Trig, Lena pulled that muscle days ago during a workout session she wasn't supposed to be doing. It's taken her this long to admit that she needs it looked at.'

'Couldn't Trig have just taken her to the hospital and *had* it checked out, regardless?'

'Maybe if Lena was twelve and Trig was her father,' said Poppy dryly. 'Lena's an adult of sound mind, Sebastian. If she doesn't want to see a doctor she doesn't have to see a doctor. Just ask her. Besides, Trig's caught between wanting to wrap her up in cotton wool and knowing that he'll lose her if he does.'

'Poor bastard,' murmured Seb.

'Cherished bastard,' she countered quietly. 'Trig's family, Seb. And his natural instinct is to protect. What happened at the door…he was doing a threat assessment, that's all. Nothing personal.'

'If you say so.'

'I say so,' she said with a gamine smile. 'So cut him some slack and I'll make sure he cuts you some.'

'He minds you, does he?'

'Well, he tries.'

Seb smiled. He liked the dynamic she shared with her sister and with Trig. It spoke of pushing and pulling and a robustness he hadn't expected. Not shy around family, but loving and beloved.

'I'll try too,' he murmured angelically. 'Trouble is I'm drawn to sin.'

'Aren't we all.' Her gaze locked with his and there was knowledge in those blue depths now, a knowledge that he'd put there and that he had every intention of expanding on.

Somewhere a door closed. Seb wrenched his attention away from Poppy's face and the smile in her eyes and looked towards the lounge area.

'They've gone,' she murmured.

So they had.

'I really should shower,' she said next. 'I'm all pool salty. You probably don't want me all pool salty.'

He wanted her any way he could get her.

'How long are you here for?' she asked as he took her hand and tugged her towards him.

'I have to be back in Darwin tomorrow. I'm supposed to be there now.' He bent his head and touched his tongue to her collarbone. 'The pool salt doesn't bother me.' He pulled back to look at her and she looked back in silence, her eyes slightly dazed. And then he kissed her again and this time he let the hunger come.

Her fingers were at his shirt buttons in moments. A quick tug on her bikini ties and the twin scraps of material covering her breasts were gone.

'I'm guessing that this is the insatiable-for-each-other stage of a relationship,' she said and cried out as he hoisted her in his arms and headed for the nearest private space, which just so happened to be the pantry. 'There are bedrooms,' she said next. 'Many, many bedrooms. Mine would be the one at the end of this wing on your right.'

The wing in question was a thousand miles long, or so it seemed to Seb. He had to stop and pin her against the wall as he stripped her bikini bottoms off. His shoes and trousers went at around about the same time they hit the carpet runner, Seb on his back and Poppy slick and wet all over him.

'Condom,' he said raggedly, and fitted one on and Poppy smiled a little ruefully and then straddled him again and before the kiss she bestowed on him was done he'd pushed his way inside her, all hurry and no finesse.

He wondered if he was being too rough for her, but her lips were curved and her eyes were glazed as he withdrew and pulled her to her feet again. In his arms with her legs wrapped around his waist as he positioned her for entry and thrust into her again.

'More,' she gasped, and then again as he backed her against a wall and thrust harder.

'Better,' she whispered and then bit down on his ear and then laid waste to his mouth and by the time they made it to her bedroom and her bed, it was all he could

do to fall down on it with her and give himself over to
her assault.

'Don't you be careful with me this time,' she muttered fiercely, so Seb wasn't, and she was wild beneath
him, and utterly unafraid of where it might lead. He
went down on her again and gloried in her sweetness,
licking into her and over her and then sucking hard as
she cried out and bucked beneath his ministrations. Not
like last time, not gentle and measured, but reckless and
raw in his need to possess.

He brought her to completion that way, and while
she still rode the waves he knelt up and got behind her
and slid into her again and slipped a finger either side
of her jutting little clitoris. And with her eyes closed
and her breath coming in gasps as she leaned back into
him, he made her come again.

He could do anything with her, she was that responsive. But she had a mind and she reclaimed it eventually as he slowed his strokes and slipped out of her
completely. Still hard, still straining but he wanted her
in a different way now. He needed to see her face, and
he needed her beneath him, with her hands above her
head and her fingers clenched around his.

Like that. Just like that, as she picked up his rhythm
and made it theirs alone. Slow, deep strokes and kisses
hot and wet, a deep, drugging ecstasy and finally, as
she climaxed around him yet again, a shattering, soul-
screaming release.

CHAPTER NINE

POPPY woke before dawn the next morning, with a sleeping Seb wrapped around her. He'd taken most of the bed, she'd taken most of the covers, and her heart stuttered as he pressed a kiss to her temple and his arm tightened around her momentarily before he loosened his grip and slid back into sleep.

The man was tired and so he should be. Poppy was tired too, but she'd remembered that their clothes were out there somewhere and that it wouldn't hurt to have them in *here*.

She slipped on the pearly grey shortie nightie that she usually slept in and slipped out of the room and closed the door silently behind her. The first item she picked up was a black sock. The sock monster had already visited because there didn't seem to be another. Poppy scooped up boxers, then trousers, shoes—there were two of those—bikini bottoms. Seb's shirt would be where? In the pantry?

But it wasn't.

In the kitchen?

Nope. But Trig was.

He sat at the breakfast bar, bare-chested and fresh from either a shower or a swim. He had a very nice chest; Poppy had always thought so. But the difference between looking at a bare-chested Trig and a similarly undressed Sebastian was enormous.

With Trig there was no fierce quickening of blood and of breath. No overwhelming need to touch him and taste him. Good to know that she had not turned into a nymphomaniac overnight. That her complete sexual abandon happened in the presence of one man and one man only.

Trig's gaze rested thoughtfully on the pile of clothes in her arms as he reached for the cereal box and filled his bowl to the brim with flakes of corn. Two litres of skim milk sat beside him, awaiting annihilation.

'Morning,' she said warily, for he had a look in his eyes that didn't bode well for someone, and she had a feeling that someone was her.

'Laundry day, is it?' he asked silkily, and then reached down to the barstool beside him and lifted up her bikini top, dangling it from his fingertips. 'Guess you'll be needing this, then.'

Poppy fought a blush and failed. The sooner she stopped blushing altogether, the better. She was in complete agreement with Seb on that one.

'Thank you,' she murmured and moved to take it, only to have him whip it out of her reach. Her hands were already full of clothes and shoes and her reach was limited.

'Adrian.' Poppy narrowed her gaze. She wasn't impressed. 'Give.'

'What do you know about him, Poppy?' Clearly, Trig's honorary big brother status was not just an empty title as far as he was concerned.

'I know he pleases me.'

'In bed? It's not as if you have a lot to compare him with.'

'Are you berating me for falling into bed with him so fast? Or am I to infer from your comment that you think I should have fallen into bed with a dozen others before him?'

Trig looked momentarily confused and Poppy took the opportunity to snatch her bikini top from his unwary fingers. 'Sebastian Reyne pleases me. Both in bed and out. I've waited a long time to be able to say that about a man, Adrian. A very long time.'

'Point taken, but he comes in here and—'

'And what? Challenges you? Lays claim to me? You'd think less of him if he didn't.'

'He's going to be a possessive man, Poppy.'

'And?'

'And you're going to get sick of it.'

'When and *if* I do, I will deal with it. Quite frankly, I don't see him as any more possessive than, say, you, or Jared, or Damon. Do you really think me incapable of holding my own with any of you?'

'I was just—'

'Don't.'

'—making an observation.'

'Based on a three minute introduction. And maybe you're right. And maybe you haven't even tried to get to know him yet. Maybe you'd think more of him if you did.'

She might not have spoken her thoughts aloud every time she'd had them but Poppy had *always* known her own heart and mind. Fight for a cause or fight for a man—she'd been raised with warriors and, although she'd chosen a gentler, more peaceful path through life, her fighting colours were no different from theirs.

'I'm not a mouse,' she told Trig fiercely. 'I know what I want and right now I want Seb to feel welcome here. The way I see it, you can either help me in that regard or, so help me, I will crucify you.'

Poppy turned on her heel; she'd made her point and had no intention of repeating it.

'Poppy,' said Trig when she was halfway across the kitchen.

'What!' It was a mark of iron-willed self-control that her voice was still low, especially when she saw Seb's white shirt in Trig's outstretched hand.

'You might want to take this too.'

Seb opened his eyes when Poppy came back into the bedroom, possibly because she hadn't been quite so quiet in her door handling procedures as she'd been when she left. It took a lot to get her riled, but Trig had managed it effortlessly.

Cookies for him.

'Are you going to be a possessive man?' she said as she dumped the clothes on the bed and promptly crawled on top of a hot and naked Seb and pinned him to the bed with her weight.

'Where you're concerned?' he murmured and shifted beneath her, his hands sliding to her waist and his thumbs tracing lazy circles there. 'Looks like. Let me guess. You ran into Trig.'

'He thinks you're going to be possessive,' she repeated. 'Which could prove a problem given that I already have two brothers who can be more than a touch protective at times, then there's Trig who considers himself an honorary brother and is just as bad, and then there's Lena, who I guarantee will offer to cut out your heart if you hurt me.'

'Really?' Seb smiled that lazy smile. 'How is Lena this morning?'

'Dammit!' She'd forgotten to ask. 'Don't move.'

So it was back through the clothing free hallway again and into the kitchen where Trig sat eating his cereal.

'Is this a rerun?' he asked warily. 'Because if it is, I like your new friend. Must ask him where he buys his shirts.'

'He asked me how Lena was,' said Poppy curtly. 'And I didn't know.'

That shut breakfast boy's smart mouth up. He put down his spoon. 'The doctors are pretty sure it's just a muscle tear, but they looked at Lena's last lot of X-rays and they've decided to take a new set. She's booked in for Thursday. They gave her better painkillers and ordered bed rest until further notice. She's asleep.'

'You double dosed her?'

'No, but she topped herself up with the new ones at three this morning. They work a treat.'

'And you know this how?'

'I was sitting in a chair beside her bed playing Florence goddamn Nightingale,' he said, and in a rougher, softer voice, 'She had my hand, Pop. She wouldn't let it go.'

'Oh.' Poppy blinked hard at the image that came to mind. Of Lena vulnerable and Trig standing guard over her. She leaned across the counter and pressed a kiss to his forehead. 'Thank you. Maybe you should try and get some sleep this morning too.' She turned to go.

'Poppy,' murmured Trig as she reached the door and

she turned towards him warily. She didn't want to be at odds with Trig, she really didn't, but if he was going to offer up some new character assassination of Sebastian, they would be.

'Point for Seb.'

'Lena's dosed up on painkillers and asleep in her room,' Poppy said as she straddled Seb's naked form and settled down atop him. 'Trig's going back to bed for a nana nap if he knows what's good for him.'

'Do they *know* you rule them all, yet? Do they realise how strong-willed you are?' His hand slipped over her stomach, wide and warm.

Poppy smiled, wide and easy. 'Why, Sebastian? Are you calling me a tyrant?'

'I wouldn't dare,' he murmured. 'I was merely making the observation that more often than not, and with seeming effortlessness on your part, people around you tend to do what you want them to do. There's no conflict, no apparent manipulation.'

'It's a gift.'

'It's frightening,' he muttered. 'Look at me. Did I intend to deflower my brother's boss? No. Did I intend to end up on your doorstep yesterday? No.'

'Why *did* you end up on my doorstep yesterday?' Poppy leaned forward to nibble at his lips.

'You mean besides this?' He deepened the kiss and a now familiar tightness began to spread deep in her belly.

'Yes.' She let him move on to graze the cord of her neck. 'Besides this.'

'I'd seen Bonnie,' he offered gruffly. 'I'd given her the picture.' His lips found the sensitive spot behind her ear. 'After that, all I wanted to do was to see you.

I haven't finished with you yet, Ophelia. Not by a long shot.'

He could make love to her with words, this man, just as easily as he made love to her with his body. The effect was the same. She melted for him. Because of him. And he grew hard beneath her and she set her hands to his shoulders and let the silk of her panties provide a little extra slide as she pressed down against him. 'You are so easy,' he whispered.

'You are so wrong.' Poppy closed her eyes and began to move, not sure she would ever get her fill of this man's body and the pleasure it could bring to hers.

'You're easy for me.'

Oh. 'Yes. Well.' He rolled her onto her back beneath him, which was exactly where she wanted to be this morning. 'True.'

'What am I going to do with you?'

'This,' she suggested shamelessly. 'A lot.'

They made it to brunch, and were greeted by a relentlessly polite Trig and a still drowsy Lena. Trig had taken charge of the kitchen, but he was all about sharing the joy as he set Poppy to slicing watermelon for a fruit platter. Lena was in charge of toast.

'Tongs,' murmured Seb as Trig held them out to him.

Trig pointed in the direction of the pan. 'I'm giving him my tongs, Poppy. I'm putting him in charge of the bacon and eggs. It's an act of pure trust and acceptance. Gestures don't come any more welcoming than that.'

'Or more trumpeted,' murmured Lena.

'Why, thank you, Adrian.' Poppy favoured Trig with a gentle smile. 'What are you going to do now that you've assigned all the jobs?'

'I'm going to make coffee. I'm going to give one to my new acquaintance here, while I keep an eye on him to make sure he doesn't burn the bacon. Then I'm going to ask him what happens on an offshore oil rig once there's been a blowout. Rest easy, Pop. I'm not even going to try and list your faults; the primary one being that even though you rarely set your sights on something, the minute you do it's as good as a done deal. I'm not even going to bother telling him to run.' Trig turned to Seb with an air of gleeful enjoyment. 'You *can* run, right?'

'Put a man on a gushing rig and there *is* nowhere to run,' countered Seb. 'You get your hard hat on, ante up and prepare to get well and truly worked over.'

'Then what happens?' asked Lena.

'Then you hit that wilful mother with everything you've got.'

'Mothers, eh? Hear that, Poppy?' asked Lena dryly. 'Wilful oil-wells are female. Tell me, Sebastian—do they become male if they behave?'

'They're always female.' Seb shot Lena an unrepentant smile. 'Just ask anyone who's ever worked on one.'

'Lena's going to want your balls for breakfast soon, my new friend,' said Trig. 'Me, I'm liking you more and more.'

'So you're on a rig in the middle of the ocean and it's raining oil and spewing gas and you're hitting that wilful mother with everything you've got,' murmured Lena, her eyes alight with laughter. 'Then what happens?'

'Simple. You fight until you win.'

Seb needed to leave for Brisbane after brunch was over. He needed to get to the plane in order to get to Darwin and the work he'd left behind. Poppy saw him to the car with a mixture of contentment and sadness. They were in a better place with their relationship than they had been when they'd parted two days ago. The footing was firmer, their understanding of each other more secure. There was still the small matter of Poppy living in and working out of Oxford at this point in time and Sebastian working out of Darwin, but the tyranny of distance was hardly an insurmountable object when money was plentiful and transport so readily available.

'You going to come visit me before you leave?' he asked her as they stood beside the hire car.

'What would I do there?'

'Whatever you want. I can show you round. Show you what I do, introduce you to the crew. I'm not sure who's there at the moment. Not everyone.'

'Is this your equivalent of taking me to meet your mother?'

'Close. You want to meet my mother too?'

'I've met her. Tom brought her and your father in to work one day when they were visiting the UK.'

'Perfect,' said Seb. 'You're already done.'

'This is going to get messy,' she murmured. 'Tom's going to—'

'Vie with Lena for best threat if I do anything to hurt you. Honestly, he'll enjoy himself.' But Poppy didn't smile. Seb sighed. 'We're good together, Poppy, but we've been living on an island. Possibly in a bar. All I'm asking is do you want to continue this in real life? If you do…' Seb shrugged and tried to look cool, calm and collected. 'The invitation's there.'

* * *

'He wants me to meet his crew,' said Poppy to Lena and Trig once she'd stepped back inside. 'It's too soon. Don't you think it's too soon?'

Lena eyed Poppy thoughtfully. 'Judging from the afterglow you've got going on there, I'm going to have to go with no.'

'He's worried that I'm not going to fit.'

'He said that?'

'Well, no. But he should have.'

'Are *you* worried that you're not going to fit?' asked Lena gently.

'A little.' Poppy took a breath and let the terror she'd been holding at bay come. 'A lot. And it's not that they're going to be rowdy or rough, it's just…'

'People,' Trig finished for her.

'Exactly. I'm no good with people. Especially large groups of people I've never met before and badly want to impress.'

'But you are good with Seb,' said Lena thoughtfully. 'You're very good with him.'

'Yes, and it took a deserted island, a tiger shark, bribery, corruption, a code I couldn't crack and half a dozen blackouts to get that way with him. I'm going to muck it up. I know I'm going to muck it up.'

Lena sighed. Trig said nothing.

'This is where you say, "No, you won't, Pop,"' said Poppy helpfully.

'No offence, Pop,' offered Trig, 'but I've watched you turn into wallpaper in the company of strangers for close to thirty years now. Just tell him you'd rather meet them one on one, maybe a year apart.'

'I don't think it's going to work that way, Trig,' said Lena, fine frown lines forming between her eyes.

'Poppy says his company started out as an offshore rig troubleshooting crew. They're tight. Almost an assault team. Total trust. He's not going to be able to back off from them in order to accommodate Poppy's neuroses. He needs her to be able to cope with them and the work they do. I'm betting he's had women turn tail and *run* once they're exposed to his world.' Lena turned to Poppy. 'You can stay a little bit reserved. You always do. But you're going to have to cope.'

'I know.' Poppy looked past the pool, past the garden to the beach and ocean beyond. Sink or swim. 'It's a test.'

Poppy dithered for an afternoon, stared at the airline company's website for far too long, and then finally pressed the confirm button on a flight to Darwin and then another flight from Darwin to London via Singapore. The following day she found herself in Darwin. Stinking hot and still only nine in the morning, but the views over the red channel country of Northern Australia had been spectacular, and she'd have travelled a lot further to feel the utter contentment she'd felt when Seb had wrapped his arms around her at the airport and just stood there.

'I fly on to London tomorrow,' she murmured when finally he let her go. 'I need to get back.'

'I'll get you back here in time to catch that flight,' he told her. 'I'm not asking you to neglect your work in my favour. Much. I just need you to know what you're getting into. With me. Before we get in too deep.'

Poppy could have told him it was already too late, that she was already in too deep, but she held her tongue

as they walked through the car park and he handed her
into a Land Cruiser and drove her to his apartment.

Nice place. Lock on the door for which the man had
keys. He liked comfort and had the money to make it
happen, but she'd known all that from her stay on the
island. No surprises for Poppy there. 'My Oxford flat's
a lot smaller,' she said as he showed her around. 'Just
so you know.'

'Smaller can be better,' he murmured. 'Sometimes.'
Not something he had to worry about, though, and his
smile said he knew it. 'You want the bedroom tour next
or the workplace one?'

'Is that really a question?

Apparently it wasn't. They did the bedroom tour first
and only after they were sated did Sebastian sit up with
a groan, scrub at his face and say he had to go to work
and did she want to come and see it and then maybe
head off and do some solo sightseeing while he put in
a few hours' work. Or she could stay here and suit herself. Or borrow his car and go where she would. No
pressure, but he had to put in an appearance at work.

So she went with him to work and it didn't take a genius to figure out that Seb was pleased by her decision.

Step one: commit to taking a tour through his world.
Step one had been accomplished. Step two: impress the
people who inhabited Seb's world, and if she couldn't
quite manage that, she'd settle for having them not think
she was a freak. Lena had given her a whole list of plati-
tudes and Poppy ran through every one of them in her
head as she and Seb walked towards a low-set cream-
coloured building that backed onto a marina.

'More boats,' she murmured. Just what she needed.

'Get you where you're going, though, don't they?' he countered with a wry grin.

'Just for the record, this visit to your world doesn't involve a trip to an offshore oil rig, does it? Because while Trig may have expressed delight at the notion, I, on the other hand, am quite happy to look at some pictures, fire up the imagination and take it from there.'

'Ladies' choice,' he said, and pushed open the heavy glass door and ushered her inside.

Sebco's Darwin base had a wickedly expensive-looking conference room as its showpiece. The conference room was empty. Poppy liked it at once. Alas, the workplace tour got a whole lot more complicated after that. Admin areas, monitoring areas, planning and design areas, Wendy's area.

Wendy of telephone fame. The one who'd got a whole lot friendlier once Poppy had mentioned that she was a friend of Seb's *brother*. Using Wendy's phone voice and manner as her reference point, Poppy had imagined the woman as some kind of cross between Mae West and Margaret Thatcher, and she wasn't far wrong.

Wendy was gimlet of eye, grey of hair and gave off the unmistakeable vibe of a woman who didn't take orders from anyone.

'Hello, Poppet,' said Wendy.

'Poppy,' said Poppy. 'Or Ophelia.' Wendy's eyebrows went up. 'West.'

'The one from the island?' said Wendy. 'Tom's friend?' But this time, Wendy did not grow more friendly by the moment. 'How'd you get Seb to give you the tour?'

'I, ah, don't know,' said Poppy. Had Sebastian not told them she was his...whatever she was? Obviously not. 'He just offered.'

'Yeah, well, he usually knows better.' Wendy fixed Seb with a glacial glare. 'You have a meeting with Roan Corp at 2:00 p.m. There's a report on your desk and unless you want to get screwed over, well and good, I suggest you get your head back in the game and read it. Don't say I didn't warn you.'

'The Roan Corp meeting's off unless they agree to the list of contract amendments I sent through to them this morning before you got to work. If they want more time, give them two days. If they can't get back to us by then, blow them off.'

'Oh,' said Wendy. 'My pleasure. Joel's in, and he wants to see you. He's going over the Carter rig's maintenance schedules again.'

'Why?'

'No idea. No one tells me anything around here. It's enough to make a woman quit. But I suggest you get in there and ask the man what his problem is fairly soon, because if you don't he's going to blow. You're not the only one who took Cam's death hard.'

'You sound busy,' said Poppy to Seb. 'There's no need to give me the tour. I can just go.'

'Car keys,' said Seb and handed them to Poppy. 'House keys as well. If I'm not back in fifteen minutes, leave without me. I'll meet you back at home.'

Seb left. Poppy stayed. Wendy stared.

'Is the Carter rig the one the accident took place on?' asked Poppy.

'Know about that, do you?'

Poppy didn't know how to answer that one, so she said nothing. Had Seb spoken to her in confidence about it? Were people supposed to know anything about it?

Poppy didn't know. She didn't know what to do with Seb's car keys either.

'Tom around?' asked Wendy.

'Tom's in London.'

'But he was with you on the island.'

'No. Tom's a work colleague,' offered Poppy. 'I just borrowed the island for a bit. He and I aren't close in the way you might be thinking.'

'And you and Seb?'

'Met last week.' What was she supposed to say? That she'd met and fallen in love with him within a week? That she was now his girlfriend? Seb wasn't here to guide her and he certainly hadn't told Wendy anything about her so Poppy erred on the side of caution. 'He's a good host.'

Wendy looked at Seb's keys and her lips narrowed.

'Does Seb have an office I could wait in?' asked Poppy. 'I don't want to interrupt you.'

'Second door on the right. Make yourself at home.'

Poppy found Seb's office, shut the door behind her with a gentle click and closed her eyes. So Wendy wasn't shaping up to be a big Poppy fan. Nothing to worry about. She headed for the visitors' chair at Seb's desk and sank into it. Paperwork covered most of the table. Some sort of data printout, by the looks of it.

She tried ignoring it. She tried estimating the area of the wall, based on the number of concrete bricks. But the data just kept calling to her and eventually she turned it round and took a look. Hydrostatic pressure. Drill rates. Flow rates. Pipe weights. Times.

Interesting.

At some point she must've picked up a pencil.

Because that was how Seb found her. Knee deep in data and running averages in her head.

'Hi,' she said.

'Joel Grainger, meet Poppy West,' said Seb, his gaze sliding from her to the data stream and back. 'Poppy works with my brother.'

'The mad genius?' said Joel.

'She's his boss.'

'She's nosey,' said Joel.

'I was just passing the time.' Poppy looked to Seb. 'I really should go. You're busy.' He hadn't introduced her as his girlfriend. Why hadn't he introduced her as his girlfriend? Was it implied? Was she supposed to do something non-verbal like kiss him on the cheek on the way out the door? She didn't know. She never knew these things.

'Let me show you round first, then you can go,' said Seb. 'No point dragging you here for nothing. Ten minutes.'

Partner Joel scowled but Seb was unruffled. So it was meet the rest of the admin staff—three women and two men. Smile. And then meet the engineers— only three of them in the complex this morning. Smile. While Poppy's palms grew damper and her face began to freeze.

This place was jam-packed with vibrant, squabbling people and Poppy was not one of them. Warm smiles turned cooler at the stiffness of her responses. Seb's gaze turned sharper and he rubbed at her back as if to warm her up.

'Need some coffee?' he asked finally, because it had become blatantly obvious that she sure as hell needed something to get her through this meet and greet.

'And a bathroom. Please.'

A short time later Poppy stood in the three-cubicle ladies' room staring at the watchful, blue-eyed woman in the mirror. So far not good, but there was still time to relax and mingle and make a good impression.

She went into the centre stall and shut the door and put the lid down and then sat down and closed her eyes. *Ask someone a question about themselves or their work. Pick a friendly face and flirt. Well...not flirt, exactly, but open up and be responsive.*

Fight her innate fear of being labelled outcast, because outcast was what she'd be if she couldn't change her ways.

Time to go, but then the outer ladies' room door creaked and Poppy heard footsteps and chatter.

About her.

'Hasn't got much to say, has she?' said one voice. 'Wonder what Seb sees in her?'

'Pretty face,' said another voice.

'Yeah, but boring clothes,' said the first voice. 'Skinny too. I thought Seb went for curves.'

'Guess he's changed diets,' said the other voice. 'Wendy says she's some kind of brain. Maybe she's intellectually stimulating.'

'For that she'd have to talk.'

Someone laughed. 'Wait till Roarke gets a load of her. Reckon he'll make good on his promise to steal Seb's next woman?'

'Technically, it was not Seb's fault that Roarke's weekend fling took one look at Seb and wanted to trade up. Seb never touched her. All he did was expose her for the money-grubbing little whore she was.'

Whoa. Not exactly inclined to mince words, these two.

Poppy leaned forward and stared at her shoes as the women occupied stalls either side of her.

She could still do this. She could.

She hit the flush button, gave her hands the fastest wash in history and went to find Seb.

She wasn't coping. And Seb didn't know if it was because she hated his world and the people in it or because of her innate reserve and shyness, but the woman who'd enslaved his body and captured his soul was drowning in a sea of people and they hadn't even noticed.

He went with instinct as he went to her and handed her his coffee. She eyed him uncertainly. 'About that data set in your office,' she said. 'Was it from the well that blew?'

Seb nodded.

'Does it tell the right story?'

'What do you mean?'

'I noticed a lot of trends in the data.'

'There are. That's what we monitor. Trends help predict kicks and other issues.'

Joel had come upon them again. Seb hadn't cottoned on to what it was that was bothering Joel yet, but he would, and soon. Poppy gave the man an uncertain smile.

'I'd like to have another look at the data, if I could,' she told Seb, continuing the conversation. 'And the programming behind it.' Burying herself in maths again because she didn't know how to deal with people. On the other hand, if focusing on the work helped her find her feet in this environment, Seb was all for it.

'Why?' asked Joel.

'The hydrostatic pressure calculations towards the end of that data set were so consistent. Be good to know why.'

'Because the well was being controlled,' snapped Joel.

'I think it's worth another look.'

'Are you serious?' said Joel. 'Is she serious?'

'Usually,' said Seb.

'And you're actually going to indulge her? When did she become the expert? When did *you* stop leading with your head?'

'It's not as if you have anything to lose,' said Poppy coolly.

Joel glared at her, and then turned on his heel and strode from the room.

Seb sighed and ran a hand through his hair. 'Actually, he does. Joel's the software engineer for our data monitoring systems. That's his baby you want to examine.'

'Oh.' Poppy shot him a glance full of apology. 'I didn't realise I was treading on toes. Still.'

'You'll get the data, Poppy. But I'd better go and speak to him. I still don't know what's eating him. Something sure as hell is.'

Poppy nodded, but not before he'd seen the brief flash of outright terror in her eyes.

'Go,' she said.

'You'll be all right here for five minutes?'

'Of course.'

He wanted to believe her.

'Go,' she said gently.

'If a man called Roarke comes in, he's probably going to try and come on to you,' said Seb. 'It's a long story. I'd kill him but he's saved my life a couple of times and I love him, so you're going to have to make him see the error of his ways on your own.'

Poppy nodded. 'Okay.'

Seb left after that.

Poppy took a calming breath and pretended herself back on the island. Nothing but the clouds in the sky and the sun on her face. No people to insult. No one to judge her. No vengeance-motivated suitors.

And then a man entered the room and he was big, bald and beautiful and people smiled when they saw him.

'Someone told me our fearless leader had brought a woman with him to work,' he said to the room at large. 'I'm here to collect.'

Someone sniggered, nameless others smiled. Every eye seemed to be upon her.

'You can try,' said a voice. 'Twenty says you've got no chance.'

'I'll take that bet,' said another voice.

'Don't you worry about them,' said a woman as she rinsed her coffee cup in the nearby sink and set it on the drying rack. 'They just like to play.' And with a wink, 'I've got ten over here that says Roarke won't get more than two words out of her.'

'What are the two words?'

And then the big man who'd started it all caught her gaze and smiled and headed her way.

'Name's Roarke,' he said when he reached her.

Of course it was. 'Ophelia.'

'Ophelia,' he rumbled. 'Pretty. Do you like your men rich? I'm rich.'

'I have money,' she murmured. 'It's not a prerequisite.'

'Damn. That one usually works. Do you like them unencumbered? I'm currently unencumbered.' And quite possibly stark raving mad. 'I learned that phrase from Seb,' he added smoothly. 'He was currently unencumbered when he stole my date.'

'Always the gentleman,' murmured Poppy.

'I'm bigger than Seb,' offered Roarke next. 'In every way.'

'Wrong,' said a voice.

Poppy really didn't want to dwell on how that laughing voice knew such intimate details.

'I'm not Seb's date,' she said, hoping it might make the devilish Roarke go away.

'You have his car keys.'

'Yes, and I'm about to use them.'

'Eye gouge,' said a different voice.

'Bet,' said another.

'As in get in the car and drive away,' said Poppy.

'Any message you'd like me to give Seb?' asked Roarke. 'You took one look at me and knew it would never work out between the two of you? I'd be happy to tell him that.'

'Just—'

Poppy glanced round at the sea of faces and it wasn't malice she saw in them, it was just—with this lot it was either sink or swim.

'I'm sorry,' she mumbled and handed him Seb's coffee cup. 'Just tell him I had to go.'

Poppy sat in the dimly lit coffee shop and stared unseeingly at the magazine lying open on the table top. Her trip to Seb's workplace had been a complete failure, on so many levels. She'd antagonised his software engineer, failed to impress his office manager—or anyone else. And then there'd been the debacle in the staff room. The charming Roarke who hadn't really been trying to pick her up at all—she'd had all the warning in the world that he was just playing, they were *all* just playing, and *surely* she could have played along too until Seb got back.

Surely she could have found some wit and panache from somewhere.

But she hadn't.

Instead, the mouse had won the day and Poppy had gone into hiding. Nursing her social inadequacies here in the light of the tropical afternoon sun.

What time was Seb likely to finish work? Poppy's wristwatch said four-thirty. Soon?

She'd have to face him soon.

And then she would see in his eyes that she didn't fit in his world and that he was reconsidering his options when it came to continuing their relationship.

Who'd blame him?

An even deeper shadow fell across the table and Poppy looked up to see Wendy from Seb's office, and her eyes were shrewdly assessing.

'Mind if I join you?' asked Wendy.

Politeness warred with honesty. Wendy's eyes narrowed and politeness won. 'Feel free.'

Wendy took a seat. 'You're a hard woman to find.'

'You found me,' countered Poppy. 'How did you find me?'

'Saw the car on my way to the post office.'

'Oh.'

'Seb's been trying to phone you all afternoon.'

'I don't have a phone on me at the moment. It's probably at his place.'

'Yeah, he left messages there too.'

'Oh.'

'Care for a rundown on what happened after you left?' asked Wendy. 'Let's see, Seb pulled all the engineers and half the admin staff off their jobs and set them to breaking down the Carter rig data and putting it back together again, with Joel arguing black and blue that he'd already done it, only they did it alongside a review of the maintenance log this time, which pointed them towards a faulty valve, which was buggering up the pressure readings, at which point everybody said Hallelujah because they now know what caused the blowout and it wasn't human error on their part. That took most of the day, by the way. Sebastian seemed to think you'd have figured it out in two minutes flat had he given you another run at the data, but fortunately the only person he said that to was me. Trust me, it was better that they got to the bottom of this one by themselves. This one was personal.'

'I get that,' said Poppy.

'So what else happened?' said Wendy. 'Oh, yeah. The *other* incident in the staff room. The one that happened after you'd left. Seb came back and found you gone and Roarke grinning. A mistake Roarke compounded by telling Seb you'd told the staff room at large that you weren't Seb's girl.'

'I said that?'

'Apparently. Never seen a man go so still and calm with quite that degree of murder in his eyes. All bets were off. Not sure anyone was even breathing.'

'And?' said Poppy.

'And what?' asked Wendy blandly.

'What happened next?'

'My guess is that Roarke figured out between one heartbeat and the next just how gone Seb was on you, because he apologised at once and told Seb that he'd find you and bring you back. To which Seb replied leave it. Not that anyone did. A dozen people have been tag-teaming trips to Seb's apartment all afternoon in the hope of finding you there. Amateurs.'

'If you say so.'

'What you may not realise yet about Seb, given that you've known him for all of a week, is that he doesn't place much value on himself as a partner. Takes a special type of woman to deal with the level of risk Seb's comfortable with. Seb knows that. Which means that if a woman wants to walk away he lets them.'

'And you're telling me this why?'

'Because I have this sinking suspicion that he's going to let you walk away too. From what he perceives as his flaws. And I'm not sure that's why you ran. I think *we* scared you off. The people you met today rather than the nature of the work itself. You walked into a world of frustration, what with Seb having been away and the cause of the blowout still uncertain. You got drawn into undercurrents you couldn't have known about. People trying to let off a bit of steam. It wasn't our finest moment. And I just want you to know that we can do better by you if you'll give us another chance.'

'What makes you think I won't blow that chance too?' asked Poppy, anxiety riding her hard. 'I'm not good with people. I miss my cues. I do my pastel best to turn into wallpaper. I *begged* Seb to teach me how to have a conversation with a man. We practised in an imaginary bar.'

'Seriously?'

'Seriously. Chances are, Seb's going to be glad to see the *end* of me. Who wants to be saddled with a woman who can't even manage to stand her ground for five minutes in a staff room?'

'I've explained the why of that,' said Wendy sternly. 'And I'm telling you, he laid us all to waste over our treatment of you, and he did it without uttering a word. He couldn't go after you then, because he *did* have to pick up the reins and run the bloody company. And he's not coming after you now because he's not sure if it's us you're running from or him, so we're doing something about it. Roarke's working on Seb. I drew you. Are you really going to sit here obsessing over your own insecurities and not allow Sebastian any of his own? At least give him the benefit of the doubt and go find him and see if he still wants you. Ask him straight.'

'That easy, huh?'

'I didn't say anything about easy,' snapped Wendy. 'It's about risk, and taking it. And it's about reward, and earning it. And it's about giving people another chance.'

How often had Poppy wanted other people to give *her* a chance? Too many times to count.

'I guess I should probably follow you back to Sebco now.'

'That was my first thought.' Wendy smiled archly. 'But I've since reconsidered. It's almost knock-off time. I think we can do a little better than that.'

* * *

Seb paced his office and tried not to scowl as Roarke stuck his head around the door, and then, seeing that the room was empty but for Seb, came all the way in.

'That was Wendy,' he said. 'She wants you to drop by her house on your way home.'

'What for?'

'Wants you to pick something up. Still no word from Ophelia?'

'She called. Asked if I was right for a ride home and if I was then she'd meet me back at my place.'

'See? She came back. Probably spent the day shopping.'

Or thinking up reasons not to be with him, thought Seb bleakly. She wouldn't have to think hard. 'I wish.'

'What do you wish?'

'She's not resilient enough for this kind of life, Roarke. She doesn't do risk. She's used to it from the people around her, mind, but unless she's motivated by love she's far more inclined to step away from it. She's not going to risk herself for me.'

'Have you asked her to?'

'I asked her here. For Poppy, that was risky.'

'But she did it.'

'And she fled.'

'Not entirely her fault,' Roarke muttered.

'Yeah, I got the memo.' Seb smiled humourlessly. 'I'm in love with her, Roarke. All the way gone. But I can't walk away from the life I've built here or the people in it. I can't be someone I'm not. She can't be someone she's not. Where's the middle ground?'

'There's plenty of middle ground,' said Roarke. 'Then there's her ground, and your ground, and new ground for both of you, and you've just got to find it.'

'You're almost making sense.'

'I know. I do that occasionally. So here's what you're going to do. First you find her and ask her to give your friends another chance. That's important.'

'Yeah, I can really see how that'll make her love me.'

'All right, forget that for now but make sure you come back to it later. First you find her. Take her out for dinner. Order in. Whatever. Tell her you know today didn't go so well but that practice will help. Then you step up. Fight the fear. Get her naked. And mention that you love her. Simple.'

'Simple,' said Seb.

'Fight the fear,' said Roarke with an unholy grin.

'What's with getting her naked first?'

'Incentive, man.'

'For her?'

'For you.'

Poppy was in a bar. Only it wasn't a bar exactly, it was the closed-in underneath bit of Wendy's high-set wooden house. The floor was concrete, the walls were widely spaced thin wooden slats, the doors were garage roll-a-doors and the lighting was eclectic. A naked-lady lamp. Dangling, green-hatted light bulbs over the poker table and the pool table. Fluoro strips pinned to the walls. And then there was the bar.

A long, mahogany masterpiece with brass foot rests and mirrored tiles behind it, and on the shelves behind it every alcoholic beverage known to man. There was a fridge—what self-respecting bar didn't have a fridge? There were two fridges, for there was another one over by the pool table that was largely full of beer and softs, and there were posters—one of Bo Derek and another of Jimmy Dean wearing a hat.

People had started turning up almost as soon as Poppy and Wendy had arrived, and as they walked in they shoved twenty and fifty dollar notes in a jar that sat on the bar. Some of them, Poppy had met earlier at Seb's workplace. As far as she could gather, the ones she hadn't met there were partners and spouses of the ones she had. One was a brother.

'You do this often?' Poppy asked Wendy. She and Wendy were behind the bar. Wendy was keeping her busy and introducing Poppy to everyone as Seb's friend, and making it seem easy.

'Not that often. Mostly when there's something to celebrate. When the boys come off a job. When someone has a baby. Good times. Today, we're celebrating the fact that we now know why that well blew when it did. Because it's been eating at us. Tomorrow, Seb'll set a crew to working on ways to make sure it never happens again.'

'I know.' The man was damn near perfect. 'But why your place?'

'Ah, well. You can blame my late, great husband for that because it was all his idea. He reckoned he needed to let off steam after coming in off a job. I reckoned the last thing I wanted to do was haul his lily arse around Darwin's bars the minute he got home. This was the compromise. Now it's tradition.'

'And Seb's going to be here soon, you said,' murmured Poppy.

'Roarke's bringing him.'

'Roarke.'

'Don't worry about Roarke playing games with you.

That boy can be an absolute angel when he wants to be. Tonight he wants to be, I guarantee it.'

'Does anyone ever cross you?' asked Poppy. Because as far as she could tell, Wendy's iron fist of benevolence was truly, deeply and madly impressive.

'Occasionally I lose one. Not often. OY, ROGER,' she said to a weather-beaten older man who'd anteed up to the bar. 'YOU WANT A DRINK?'

'Is she yelling at me?' he said with a wide, wicked smile. 'IS SHE YELLING AT A DEAF MAN AGAIN? READ MY LIPS, WOMAN. I'll HAVE A SCOTCH.'

'Moron,' said Wendy, but she said it with affection and the Scotch she poured was from the very top shelf.

'Seb's here,' said a voice from the doorway.

'What was that?' asked Roger.

'Move over, old man,' said Wendy. 'Poppy wants to sit at the bar.'

'I do?' said Poppy.

'You said you once asked a man to teach you how to talk to strange men in imaginary bars,' said Wendy. 'I think it's time to show him what you've learned.'

Poppy scooted her way around to the other side of the bar, grateful, for once, for the company of others for they kept her hidden from Seb's view and she needed the time to compose herself. She had no idea how this was going to work but she was here, and Seb was here, and Poppy had a powerful need to prove herself capable of finding her way in Sebastian's world.

Roger eyed her curiously as she sat down and smoothed damp palms down boring beige trousers. Wordlessly, he offered her his Scotch and Poppy drank it in one long swallow.

'Roger needs another Scotch,' she said and Wendy grinned at them and poured for them both.

'I can't,' Seb was saying. 'I'm heading home.'

'One drink.'

'No.'

Then the crowd parted and Seb saw her and his mouth dropped ever so slightly open.

'What's your rush?' she asked quietly.

And Sebastian began to smile.

'Bull's-eye,' said a voice from the crowd and maybe they were talking about the dartboard and maybe not.

Seb started towards her; someone handed him a drink. These people were fun and they were flawed. Above all, they'd forged themselves a family.

'So,' he said when he reached her. 'You here alone?'

'Sort of. I've been waiting for someone to show.'

'More fool him for leaving you alone,' he said.

'Maybe he had things to do,' she murmured. 'Others to take care of first.'

'Still a fool.'

'I don't date foolish men. Life's too short. I prefer my men knowledgeable, extremely beddable and somewhat prone to taking risks.' Poppy looked him up and she looked him down. 'You're very handsome, I noticed it at once. Do you live around here?'

Green eyes and tousled black hair and a smile she fully intended to savour. 'Maybe.'

'Know any good places to eat?'

'Maybe.'

'Do you play pool?'

'I do.' Sebastian smiled. 'You?'

'Yes. We have so much in common.'

'I noticed that,' he murmured. 'What are your thoughts on deserted islands?'

'Love 'em.'

'Swimming with sharks?'

'Puppies of the sea,' she said. 'But you'll be with me, right?'

'Who wouldn't? What about men who run oil-well troubleshooting companies?'

'Heroes,' she said. 'I want one.'

'You can have me,' offered Roger, and Seb turned around to stare at him.

'Are you reading lips again?'

'Only hers,' said Roger. 'Who cares what *you're* saying?'

'Me,' said Poppy, and put her hands to Seb's broad shoulders and positioned him so that he blocked Roger from sight. 'Where were we?'

'You were after a hero,' said Seb. 'But what would you do with him?'

'Love him,' she said simply. 'A lot. Never hold him back from being who he is. Support him, should he ever need supporting.'

'He'll need it,' said Seb.

'And hope that one day he'll do the same for me. But I wouldn't want to rush him.'

'I dare say he wouldn't want to rush you either,' said Seb. 'Especially if you didn't have much experience when it came to assessing a relationship with a man. He'd try and take it slow. Give you room to move, either towards him or away. If he asked you for commitment *now*, how would you know you're making the right decision?'

'Well, there is that,' she said demurely. 'How many

relationships would you suggest a woman indulge in, in order to be considered knowledgeable enough and experienced enough to make such a swift decision? A dozen? Half a dozen?'

Sebastian scowled.

'What if she were a fast learner? It might only take three.' Poppy paused. Favoured him with a melting smile. 'What if she were a genius? Do it once, do it right. I hear that happens to them a lot.'

'Really?'

'Take it from me.' Poppy decided it was time to slip from the barstool and get up close and personal with him. One hand laying claim to his heart, the other his shoulder.

Seb's arms came around her, warm and strong. 'If she were a genius then she'd always be right,' he said. 'There'd be no living with her.'

'You'd need to factor that in.'

'I'm doing it now,' he said, and kissed her. Regardless of their audience, Poppy wound her arms around his neck and kissed him back.

'So we're in a bar,' he whispered. 'And I love you.'

'I think I could grow to like this bar,' she whispered back. 'I'm working on it.'

'I'm glad.'

'And I need you to know something.'

'What?'

'I love you too.'

* * * * *

#225 A TASTE OF THE UNTAMED
Dark, Demanding and Delicious
Susan Stephens
The playboy returns and he's looking for a wife! With sensual passion blossoming in Nacho's vineyard, can Grace resist his seduction?

#226 HIS LAST CHANCE AT REDEMPTION
Dark, Demanding and Delicious
Michelle Conder
Lexi enthralls Leo Aleksandrov with her innocence and warmth. But he has another kind of heat on his mind: the flames of passion!

#227 ONE NIGHT, SO PREGNANT!
It Starts with a Touch...
Heidi Rice
Unexpectedly expecting—not the most ideal situation for Tess Tremaine! But even less ideal? Her burning attraction to unattainable father Nate!

#228 THE RULES OF ENGAGEMENT
It Starts with a Touch...
Ally Blake
Self-confessed relationship junkie Caitlyn is going cold turkey. One fling with no strings attached is just what she needs. Enter Dax Bainbridge...

COMING NEXT MONTH from Harlequin Presents®
AVAILABLE NOVEMBER 13, 2012

#3101 BACK IN THE HEADLINES
Scandal in the Spotlight
Sharon Kendrick
From pop star to chambermaid, Roxanne Carmichael is at the mercy of the sexy Duke of Torchester—and he's proving hard to resist!

#3102 PLAYING THE ROYAL GAME
The Santina Crown
Carol Marinelli
Fact or fairy tale? Will the glamorous marriage of Allegra and Alessandro be the happily-ever-after you are expecting?

#3103 THE DANGEROUS JACOB WILDE
The Wilde Brothers
Sandra Marton
There's a thin line between antagonism and searing attraction for Addison when sparks fly between her and the scarred Jacob Wilde!

#3104 WOMAN IN A SHEIKH'S WORLD
The Private Lives of Public Playboys
Sarah Morgan
Avery Scott finds it impossible to keep things professional when she's employed by the sensual Prince Malik...the man she's never forgotten!

#3105 SURRENDERING ALL BUT HER HEART
Melanie Milburne
Natalie is trapped by Angelo Belladini in a marriage of revenge and desire. He might demand everything—but he'll never have her heart!

#3106 A ROYAL WORLD APART
The Call of Duty
Maisey Yates
Princess Evangelina and her bodyguard Mikhail must fight their passionate chemistry—until breaking from duty becomes irresistible!

REQUEST YOUR FREE BOOKS!

Harlequin *Presents*®

PASSION GUARANTEED SEDUCTION

2 FREE NOVELS PLUS
2 FREE GIFTS!

YES! Please send me 2 FREE Harlequin Presents® novels and my 2 FREE gifts (gifts are worth about $10). After receiving them, if I don't wish to receive any more books, I can return the shipping statement marked "cancel." If I don't cancel, I will receive 6 brand-new novels every month and be billed just $4.30 per book in the U.S. or $4.99 per book in Canada. That's a saving of at least 14% off the cover price! It's quite a bargain! Shipping and handling is just 50¢ per book in the U.S. and 75¢ per book in Canada.* I understand that accepting the 2 free books and gifts places me under no obligation to buy anything. I can always return a shipment and cancel at any time. Even if I never buy another book, the two free books and gifts are mine to keep forever.

106/306 HDN FERQ

Name	(PLEASE PRINT)	

Address		Apt. #

City	State/Prov.	Zip/Postal Code

Signature (if under 18, a parent or guardian must sign)

Mail to the **Reader Service:**
IN U.S.A.: P.O. Box 1867, Buffalo, NY 14240-1867
IN CANADA: P.O. Box 609, Fort Erie, Ontario L2A 5X3

Not valid for current subscribers to Harlequin Presents books.

**Are you a current subscriber to Harlequin Presents books and want to receive the larger-print edition?
Call 1-800-873-8635 or visit www.ReaderService.com.**

* Terms and prices subject to change without notice. Prices do not include applicable taxes. Sales tax applicable in N.Y. Canadian residents will be charged applicable taxes. Offer not valid in Quebec. This offer is limited to one order per household. All orders subject to credit approval. Credit or debit balances in a customer's account(s) may be offset by any other outstanding balance owed by or to the customer. Please allow 4 to 6 weeks for delivery. Offer available while quantities last.

Your Privacy—The Reader Service is committed to protecting your privacy. Our Privacy Policy is available online at www.ReaderService.com or upon request from the Reader Service.

We make a portion of our mailing list available to reputable third parties that offer products we believe may interest you. If you prefer that we not exchange your name with third parties, or if you wish to clarify or modify your communication preferences, please visit us at www.ReaderService.com/consumerchoice or write to us at Reader Service Preference Service, P.O. Box 9062, Buffalo, NY 14269. Include your complete name and address.

HP11B

When legacy commands, these Greek royals must obey!

Discover a page-turning new Harlequin Presents®
duet from *USA TODAY* bestselling author

Maisey Yates

A ROYAL WORLD APART

Desperate to escape an arranged marriage, Princess
Evangelina has tried every trick in her little black book
to dodge her security guards. But where everyone else
has failed, will her new bodyguard bend her to his
will…and steal her heart?

Available November 13, 2012.

AT HIS MAJESTY'S REQUEST

Prince Stavros Drakos rules his country like his
business—with a will of iron! And when duty demands
an heir, this resolute bachelor will turn his sole
focus to the task….

But will he finally have met his match in a world-
renowned matchmaker?

**Coming December 18, 2012,
wherever books are sold.**

* * *

"I HAVE also spoken to my parents."

"They've heard?"

"They were the ones who alerted me!" Alex said. "We have aides who monitor the press and the news constantly." Did she not understand he had been up all night dealing with this? "I am waiting for the palace to ring—to see how we will respond."

She couldn't think, her head was spinning in so many directions and Alex's presence wasn't exactly calming— not just his tension, not just the impossible situation, but the sight of him in her kitchen, the memory of his kiss. That alone would have kept her thoughts occupied for days on end, but to have to deal with all this, too…. And now the doorbell was ringing. He followed her as she went to hit the display button.

"It's my dad." She was actually a bit relieved to see him. "He'll know what to do, how to handle—"

"I thought you hated scandal," Alex interrupted.

"We'll just say—"

"I don't think you understand." Again he interrupted her and there was no trace of the man she had met yesterday; instead she faced not the man but the might of

Crown Prince Alessandro Santina. "There is no question that you will go through with this."

"You can't force me." She gave a nervous laugh. "We both know that yesterday was a mistake." She could hear the doorbell ringing. She went to press the intercom but his hand halted her, caught her by the wrist. She shot him the same look she had yesterday, the one that should warn him away, except this morning it did not work.

"You agreed to this, Allegra, the money is sitting in your account." He looked down at the paper. "Of course, we could tell the truth…" He gave a dismissive shrug. "I'm sure they have photos of later."

"It was just a kiss…."

"An expensive kiss," Alex said. "I wonder what the papers would make of it if they found out I bought your services yesterday."

"You wouldn't." She could see it now, could see the horrific headlines—she, Allegra, in the spotlight, but for shameful reasons.

"Oh, Allegra," he said softly but without endearment. "Absolutely I would. It's far too late to change your mind."

* * *

Pick up PLAYING THE ROYAL GAME by Carol Marinelli on November 13, 2012, from Harlequin® Presents®.

HPEXP1112CM